Eclipsed

The Witch's Legacy
book one
Rogue Gray

First Edition: September 2024

Major Arcana Characters

The Fool: Lucian Tattoo: A jester hat with the number 0 underneath.

The Magician: Kadence Tattoo: An infinity symbol intertwined with elemental symbols, number I engraved.

The High Priestess: River Tattoo: A crescent moon surrounded by wild dandelions with the number II.

The Empress: Karrie Tattoo: A blooming rose intertwined with vines, featuring the number III.

The Emperor: Alistair Tattoo: A jeweled crown with the number IV.

The Hierophant: Jada Tattoo: Two crossing keys above the number V.

The Lovers: Kiarra and Sage Tattoo: Intertwined hearts with number VI below.

The Chariot: Orion Tattoo: A chariot drawn by lions with number VII above it.

Strength: Kael Tattoo: A lion's head with an infinity sign.

The Hermit: Selene Tattoo: A lantern with the number IX.

Wheel of Fortune: Theo Tattoo: A spinning wheel with numbers I-X around it.

Justice: Sierra Tattoo: A silhouette of an angel blowing a trumpet with XX inscribed.

The Hanged Man: Niko Tattoo: A figure hanging upside down with number XII.

Death: Cassie Tattoo: A skeletal hand reaching for a flower, number XIII.

Temperance: Ellie Tattoo: An angel pouring water, showcasing number XIV.

The Devil: Axel Tattoo: A shadowy figure with horns, featuring number XV.

The Tower: Dominick Tattoo: A crumbling tower with people falling and flames, number XVI.

The Moon: Nyx Tattoo: A crescent moon encircled by waves with the number XVIII.

The Sun: Apollo Tattoo: A radiant sun with rays, showing the number XIX.

Judgment: Bram Tattoo: Scales holding a heart and a skull with the number XX.

The World: Thalia Tattoo: A globe embraced by laurel leaves with the number XXI.

Minor Arcana Characters

Cups

Ace of Cups: Mia Tattoo: A dove diving into a cup, symbol + above it.

Two of Cups: Ash and Amber Tattoo: Two entwined cups with number II.

Ten of Cups: Severn Tattoo: Ten cups arranged in a rainbow arc with number X.

Wands (Passion & Ambition):

Ace of Wands: Caleb Tattoo: A flame atop a wand with the number I.

Three of Wands: Rhea Tattoo: Three crossed wands with number III.

Swords (Intellect & Conflict):

Ace of Swords: Lysa Tattoo: A sword piercing through clouds, number I.

Five of Swords: Ace Tattoo: Five swords scattered chaotically, number V.

Disks

Ace of Disks: Felix Tattoo: A single disk on a pedestal, number I.

Ten of Disks: Valaric Tattoo: A tree filled with ten disk fruits, showcasing number X.

Eclipsed
   Midnight Prank

Included with the book, will be personalized songs.
Lyrics produced by yours truly. Music produced by ilove
songs. All rights reserved, and purchasing licenses have
been acquired. <3
Throughout the book there will be QR codes.

Disclaimer

The portrayal of mental illnesses, including Dissociative Identity Disorder (DID) and other related conditions in this book, is intended solely for entertainment purposes. The author does not claim to provide an accurate or comprehensive depiction of these conditions, nor should it be interpreted as a substitute for professional guidance or treatment. Readers are encouraged to seek help from qualified mental health professionals for any concerns regarding mental health.

Warning

This book contains scenes that may be disturbing to some readers. Be advised that there are descriptions of violence, including hangings, drownings, and the burning of witches, as well as other gruesome imagery. Reader discretion is strongly advised for those sensitive to such topics as well as other scenes intended for a mature audience.

ACKNOWLEDGMENTS

I want to give a big thank you to all of my readers for supporting me, and for being patient when the book was delayed! To my husband, thank you for your unconditional love and support! Without you, I would have never made it this far. You are the best! To my mom, even though you have passed on, you still live on in my heart and memory. I miss you and think of you every day. To my sister, you are my rock and I am so grateful to have you in my life. To my author friend Jeff, thank you for believing in me and reading through the roughest of my drafts. I am so thankful to have you as a friend! Lastly, to my readers, thank you from the bottom of my heart! You are the reason why I write. Your feedback means the world to me. If you have enjoyed the book, please take a moment to leave a review! They are greatly appreciated and help authors immensely.

Midnight Prank

A shrill wail cut through the night, the sound slicing into the darkness like a jagged knife. I bolted up, tangled sheets clinging to my legs as my pulse pounded in rhythm with the mismatch beat in my chest. "Lilly, knock it off," I spat into the void, only to have it echo back to me. Swallowed by the quiet that followed her chilling laughter, with palms against my ears, the whispers persisted though.

Her taunts slithered through everything—a whisper here, a giggle there—like a restless ghost I could never shake. Outside, the wind howled through the trees, branches clawing at the window, a sound that reminded me of nails being dragged across glass. Visions of her dancing beyond the shadows played in my mind. A mischievous grin painted on her face as she relished the chaos she was causing. "I know that was you," Every muscle was coiled, primed to bolt out of the cabin at any instant. Suddenly, her laughter fell silent, leaving me desperate to detect even the faintest sign of her being there.

My heart thrummed in my chest as an unsettling silence wrapped around the room. Then a flicker of movement caught my eye. A shadow darting past, quick and elusive. I rubbed my temples, as pressure built behind my eyes. "You're not real," my voice shook. *Oh, but I am.* Her voice glided through the air, soft, with a sinister undertone. Causing goosebumps to prickle along my arms. *You'll see soon enough.*

At her sinister promise, I sighed, swinging my legs over the edge of the bed. My feet touched the cold wooden floor as I clenched the blanket tighter. Hesitating momentarily, before drawing back the faded gray curtains that drape over the window. Moonlight spilled into the small room, illuminating the forest outside. Its trees were a maze of twisting shadows, and quiet chirps, and squeaks of the nocturnal life within. But just as a semblance of calm settled in, Lilly's laughter erupted again. Manic, but light, like the chime of broken bells.

Dropping the curtain helped to block out the chaos within my mind as I burrowed back under the sheets. Curling into a ball and surrendering to the allure of a dreamless sleep yet again.

The trill of my alarm sliced through the remnants of sleep, yanking me back to reality with an obnoxious insistence. Groaning, I flailed like a fish out of water, grappling with the infernal device that had declared war on my slumber. My fingers slipped over the cool surface of the clock. Until, at last, I discovered the snooze button. With a satisfying click, silence descended, thick and heavy, wrapping me in a momentary cocoon of peace. But the calm didn't last long. I flopped back onto the bed, only to feel an unsettling weight pressing against my chest—an all-too-familiar nagging sensation that I was being watched.

After an eternity of debating whether to slink off to the living room. It took a moment, but I eventually gathered the resolve to untangle from the sheets. My feet hit the floor, and I let out a sharp gasp as a chill ran up my legs. I stumbled toward the living room, plopping down on the couch. Too exhausted to bother with coffee, or anything, really. A wave of nausea rolled through me as I lay back against the cushions, taking slow, steady breaths.

My eyes wandered the living room, noticing the sun peeking out over the horizon, bathing the room in a muted gray haze, but even the faint light stung my eyes.

Blinking back the unexpected tears, I reached out in search of a pillow and buried my face in it. *Seriously, Emma? It's time to stop moping around and live a little.*

Her voice echoed in my mind, snapping me out of the haze I'd been shrouded in. I curled up tighter, the worn-out couch reminding me of better days. The once-vibrant fabric was now faded and fraying at the edges, much like my sanity. I pulled the blanket tighter around myself, hoping it could shield me from her relentless taunts. "Moping? Is that what you think I'm doing?" I buried my face deeper into the pillow.

That's exactly what you're doing, she shot back, her tone like a playful jab meant to stir the dormant anger inside. *Brooding in this empty shell of a cabin won't bring your parents back. You know that better than anyone.* I squeezed my eyes shut, trying to block the onslaught of memories—horrible snapshots that assault my mind's eye. Screeching tires, a violent crash, the suffocating silence that followed. I didn't need her prodding at those wounds.

"I know that," I managed to whisper. "But could you at least pretend you care?" *Pretending isn't my thing. You've spent every waking moment since you got here cooped up—besides your doctor visits and therapy.* "I just want to be left alone." *You and I both know that's not what you want.* The smug tone in her voice made me want to scream and strangle her all at the same time. "Just stop!" The pillow muffled my desperate shout. "Go away."

That's not going to happen, babe. We're stuck together. Might as well make the best of it. She wasn't wrong. Ever since I moved into the cabin, Lilly had been my constant companion and tormentor.

A fleck of mischief lodged within my psyche, refusing to release me. The memory of that doctor's visit would haunt me for eternity.

Four Months Prior

I perched in the office, my leg bouncing anxiously while an unsettling chill danced through the sterile air. Making the hard plastic chair beneath me feel even less comfortable. Glancing around, I noticed I was the only patient in the sterile waiting room. Only adding to the pit of unease building in my stomach. Across the room, a secretary was tapping away at her computer. Her bored expression seemingly lost in a world of endless paperwork. "Ms. Cross?" The sound of a woman's voice made me jump as my heart raced. "Yes?" I replied, trying to sound calm as the woman's gaze lingered unnervingly. She towered over me, dressed in smart black slacks and a crisp, light blue blouse.

Giving off an air of confidence I both admired and envied. Her chestnut hair was cut in a grown out pixie, with asymmetrical bangs that framed her face perfectly. I couldn't quite pin down her age. She could have been anywhere between my age–twenty–five, or even years older. She smiled warmly, holding the door open and inviting me in. "Well, Ms. Cross," she began, her tone professional yet warm. "Initially, I thought your problems stemmed from stress or anxiety. However, as I delved deeper into your case, I became increasingly concerned that there might be something more at play."

As I stepped into the room, the walls felt as though they were slowly closing in around me, her words sending a shockwave through my system. She continued before I could ask anything, however. "In reviewing your medical history, I noticed you have a lot of childhood trauma. So, after our last visit. I conducted some tests and assessments, and the results suggest that you may be experiencing symptoms of Dissociative Identity Disorder, commonly known as DID."

4

My brows furrowed, confusion flickering across my face. "This diagnosis isn't uncommon for someone with your background, but it is complex and requires specialized treatment. Let me clarify: DID occurs when a person's mind splits into two or more distinct identities. Each with its own memories and behaviors. It's essential to understand that this condition isn't a reflection of anything you did or didn't do. Rather, it can affect anyone who has gone through significant trauma and stress."

Doctor Miller was wrong. With, or without therapy, or medication. Lilly was a menace. There was no way I had created her out of thin air. I rubbed my temples, a storm gathering in the recesses of my mind as the soft flesh pulsed with life. Musty air hung thick around me, filled with the smell of damp earth and leaves that wafted in through the cracked window. However, I paused momentarily. Wondering if I had left said window open. "It smells like dirt in here." *It's fresh air. Don't be a baby,* Lilly chimed, dismissing my comment with a lightness that made me want to pull my hair out.

"Dirt isn't 'fresh air.'" With a heavy sigh, I sat up, the blanket slipping from my shoulders as I glanced around the living room again. It wasn't much, but for the past four months, it had been home—a worn couch, a cozy armchair, and an ancient wooden coffee table. This was my haven, my little piece of solitude, or it would have been if Lilly never existed.

"What time is it?" I sat up straighter, trying to wrest control back from the chaos of my mind. *A little after seven,* Lilly answered, yawning, as if to prove her point.

I guess we stayed up a little late last night, huh? "More like you kept me up." *What can I say? I was feeling chatty.* A hint of mischief laced her tone, and I could imagine her grinning from ear to ear.

"Chatty? Seriously. That's not what I'd call it." I pushed off the couch, my feet hitting the cool floor with a reluctant thud. I flexed my toes against the chill, willing myself to shake off the remnants of sleep. *Touché, darlin'.* With an exasperated huff, I trudged toward the bathroom. Half-blind and groggy, I trailed my hand along the wall, searching blindly for the light switch.

The old floorboards groaned beneath my steps. Yet when I reached the bathroom. I stopped abruptly, catching my reflection in the mirror. My eyes widened as I took in the dirt and grime plastered across my face, remnants of Lilly's nighttime escapades tangling in my hair. "What the hell?" *Oh, that.* Lilly giggled, unapologetic. *Well, I got bored, so I went on a little late-night adventure.* "What kind of adventure?" My heart raced while my panic rose. I gripped the edge of the sink, steadying myself. *Just a little stroll through the woods,* she replied airily. *You really need to go outside more. So, I figured I'd help you out.*

"This is bodily vandalism. You can't take over whenever you want." Seething, I turned the shower on. The sound of water filled the bathroom as the steam began to rise. "How many times do we have to go through this?" Silence was my only answer. It wasn't the first time Lilly had taken control while I was sleeping. I had woken up countless times covered in dirt, grime, and during other instances, things I'd rather not mention. I was beginning to think it was payback for some wrongdoing in a past life. I shook my head. "No. This is hijacking, kidnapping, or... or something equally twisted."

Oh, you know you liked it, Lilly shot back, unfazed. "Liked it?" Heat rose in my cheeks as I stepped under the stream of warm water. Letting it cascade over my body. A desperate attempt to wash away my stress and frustration. The water enveloped me, a soothing yet temporary reprieve. *I'm sorry, Em. I just get bored sometimes.* Ignoring her, I sighed as I closed my eyes. But as I did.

An unsettling image flashed through my mind—something I couldn't shake. A man, tall and blonde, lurked in the shadows of the forest.

His clothing looked as though it belonged to an entirely different era. My heart skipped a beat, and my breath caught in my throat. "What did you really do last night?" *It wouldn't be any fun if I told you.* "You didn't do anything stupid, right?" *I guess you'll find out, eventually,* she taunted, her laughter dancing at the fringes of my mind, "You're impossible."

My annoyance simmered while I tried to focus on the task at hand. I lingered in the shower, hoping to block out the chaos in my mind. Steam curled around me in soft, warm tendrils as I stepped out. Shaking off the last droplets, my mind drifted as I moved through the rest of my morning routine.

But, as I stepped into the hall, I nearly stumbled over the rug. Too engrossed in my own musings to watch my feet. I glared at it. "Could you not?" An eruption of laughter echoed through my mind again, making my insides churn. "What are you laughing at?" I asked, half-joking. *The way you're talking to inanimate objects*, she teased. *It's adorable.* "You're an inanimate object."

Oh, burn, she snickered, delighting in my frustration. Rolling my eyes, I continued down the hallway, my footsteps echoing softly as I approached my bedroom. Yet, as I neared the door, a strange smell invaded my senses. It wasn't the musty scent of damp clothes. No. It carried a distinct, horrific fragrance of fresh earth mixed with decay.

"What is that smell?" I stumbled into my cramped room, grumbling as my nose wrinkled in disgust. "Seriously, Lills, what is that smell?" I repeated, glancing around now, caught between denial and genuine concern. *I don't smell anything.* She yawned, her tone casual and nonchalant. "You're such a liar." I ran a hand through my hair, then stripped the dirty sheets off my bed. "Gross."

I tossed the dirty fabrics aside as if it could vanish with my disdain. Afterwards, I hastily pulled on a pair of jeans and a T-shirt from my reading chair. The fabric was cold against my still-damp skin, and I gathered the laundry. Taking it down the hall, I turned to the rusty old washer, still trying to find the source of the stink. *I don't have to lie,* she replied, the sarcastic glimmer evident in her tone.

"Right," I huffed. "Because lying is beneath you." Her laughter echoed in my thoughts again as I turned my attention back to the laundry. I began shaking out the clothes from the hamper, each item releasing more of the musty smell until I finally gagged, covering my mouth and nose with my shirt. "Oh my Gods, this is disgusting."

What is? Her voice takes on an innocently curious tone. "You know exactly what it is. Why don't you tell me?" My patience was running thin. *I told you, I don't smell anything.* "Ugh." Getting the truth from her was like pretending to be a dentist. I continued sorting the laundry, attempting to ignore the stench that had invaded my nostrils.

Finally, after searching for what felt like forever, I discovered the source of the smell—an old pair of tattered jeans crumpled in the corner of the hamper, the knees caked with mud and other mysterious substances—icky remnants of Lilly's excursions, no doubt. "Did you seriously wear these, get them filthy, and not wash them?" I barely managed to contain my disbelief. She didn't answer as the silence stretched between us like an unspoken accusation. "Unbelievable." I grabbed the jeans, throwing them into the washer. Hoping it would cleanse them of the horrors they had witnessed.

"I need coffee before I completely lose my shit," I muttered, storming into the kitchen, my heart pounding as I searched for relief. I swung the cabinet open, only to be met with emptiness. Not a single dish or mug in sight. "Seriously?" Frantically,

I threw open the other cabinets, each creaking door revealing an unsettling emptiness. "Where are all the dishes?" *Maybe we don't have any,* she offered nonchalantly. "We had some yesterday. They couldn't have just disappeared!" I slammed the last cupboard shut.

The sound reverberated in the quiet kitchen, only amplifying my annoyance. *Stranger things have happened.* She laughed, enjoying my confusion. I ignored her, desperation tightening my chest as I opened the silverware drawer. Empty. My mouth fell open—a reminder of my coffee-cup-less reality. "I'm going to strangle you." She remained silent. While I cursed and threatened her, I could feel the smugness radiating through our shared consciousness as I steeled myself against the counter.

"We have to replace every single dish now. Do you ever consider the consequences of your actions?" *New dishes, huh? Can I pick them this time?* I rolled my eyes, trying not to lose my sanity as she casually dismissed my scolding. "Is that why you did it? You didn't like the ones we have?" *No, I liked the ones we had. It's just that, well. You never let me buy the cutlery set with the fruit and the cheese.*

I sighed, pressing my hands against the cool countertop. "That's because they were hideous, and we wouldn't be able to return them." *But we liked them,* she insisted, her defense utterly unrealistic. "You liked them." I corrected, "that was not a 'we' moment. We had a conversation about personal boundaries."

Oh, by the way, Em? You probably shouldn't drink the coffee, and maybe even throw out the coffee maker too. Dread washed over me as I glanced at the brewing pot, the scent suddenly odd and cloying.

What did you do?" *it's not what I did, but what YOU did,* she giggled, splintering the last nerve I had left. "Oh, for fuck's sake." I slammed the lid down and threw it into the sink, watching the liquid splash and swirl in a messy surrender alongside the shards of my sanity.

Maybe next time you'll listen to me, she chirped, her playful tone stinging like a bee. I clenched my jaw, words dying on my lips. There was no use in arguing with her. She was as stubborn as I was, and I had learned long ago that engaging in these conversations only pissed me off even more.

I took a deep breath, staring at the shards of broken glass in the sink. "You're so funny," I sneered, unable to suppress the growing bitterness. *You know, you needed an upgrade anyway.* "I didn't ask for your opinion," I snapped. "I'll have to settle for instant coffee." She scoffed, and I could almost picture her rolling her eyes. *Instant coffee is for the weak.* I grabbed the jar and a spoon, not bothering with a mug. And filled a little paper cup made for mouthwash. Hoping it would turn into something remotely drinkable. "I'll make do."

I took a sip. *Oh gods, that's awful,* she groaned, her voice an echo of torture that made me smirk. "Good." I forced down every last drop, half-hoping it might finally shut her up as I tossed the spoon into the sink. *Can I drive?* "Absolutely not." *Fine. Then we better get moving,* she replied. *It's already ten, and you know how the stores get at noon.* "Yeah, yeah. Let me grab a few things."

I walked back into the living room as I grabbed my keys. She was right. If we wanted to have a chance at picking out a good set of dishes, we needed to hurry. As I stepped outside, I was met by the sun's relentless glare.

Scorching my bloodshot eyes. I squinted, trying to gather my thoughts and retain my vision. *Damn, you look like death warmed over in this lighting.* "Yeah, no thanks to you, witch," I shot back, glaring at the ground.

Oh, if you only knew the irony of that statement, my dear Em. "Whatever," I muttered, stumbling toward my old beat-up truck. Its rusted blue exterior resembles scars of endless summer days. I fumbled with the keys, trying to find the right one, with my fingers trembling from the lingering effects of the disgusting coffee.

You're going to melt in those pants. "And whose fault is that?" I growled as I slid into the truck. Leather burning through the thin fabric of my pants. *Mine.* "That's what I thought."

I shoved the key in, pumping the clutch. "Come on, Blue. Start for me," I begged, but it wouldn't comply. Sweat streamed down my forehead as the pain behind my eyes intensified into a dull ache. I took a deep breath, willing the piece of junk to comply as I tried again. Finally, the engine turned over with a sputter, and a rush of musty air greeted me from the vents. "Thank the gods," I muttered, grateful for the relief as I wiped the sweat off my brow.

Curse Of Weathersfield

The road twisted like a snake through the dense forest, sunlight breaking through the leafy canopy, casting playful patterns on the rough asphalt. Each curve offered a teasing glimpse of the tiny town waiting ahead. As I crested a rocky hill, the town unfolded before me like a postcard, with cobblestone paths weaving between quaint brick buildings adorned with rusty lanterns and faded awnings. It was almost too picturesque.

Nestled at the edge of town lay a hidden cove, hugged by steep, mossy cliffs that caught the sunlight in dappled patches. In the distance, a weathered wooden dock jutted out into the shimmering water, its planks bleached gray and worn by years of salt and sun, teetering on the brink of nostalgia. As I pulled into town, I steered my truck into the parking lot of Morbid Market. The name sent a shiver down my spine as I navigated the maze of vehicles. *Morbid Market. Fitting,* Lilly's voice dripped with sarcasm.

"You're not wrong," I muttered as the truck shuddered to a stop. Opening the door, a loud squeak echoed in the stillness—everyone in a ten-mile radius surely heard it. I hesitated, scanning the area. To my left, an elderly woman with silver hair tied into a bun, meticulously arranged antique dolls in the window of "Curios and Antiques." Their glassy eyes seemed to follow me.

Near the entrance of the Morbid Market, a bespectacled man in a tweed jacket held an armful of wilting flowers. Our eyes locked for a brief moment before he returned his focus to the drooping blooms. *Are we shopping or just people-watching today, Em?*

Lilly's impatience thrummed in my mind. "I wouldn't be here if you hadn't ruined everything," *Come on, let's go inside. You can't avoid people forever. Plus, they aren't cannibals here.* She shot back. Despite my reluctance, she was right. I couldn't hide from the world forever.

With a deep breath, I opened the truck door and stepped out. Heat rolled over me like a suffocating shroud as I crossed the parking lot. Once inside, a cool wave of air met me, giving me whiplash from the temperature change.

I took another deep breath, inhaling the mouthwatering scent of roasted chicken mingling with freshly baked bread. My stomach growled in response. A reminder that I'd skipped breakfast. Heat crept up my cheeks as the sound grew louder.

Great, exactly what I need—more attention. *Don't forget the dishes and food. We need those.* "And the coffeemaker," I added. "Now, can you be quiet? I'd rather not give people a reason to think I'm talking to myself."

As if they aren't thinking that already. Let's get the stuff and go. This place is boring. I sighed, rubbing the bridge of my nose as I navigated the aisles.

The market held a cozy yet chaotic charm, and my attention shifted to the fresh strawberries. Their sweet scent tickling my nostrils. *Those look good.* With a smirk, I picked up a container and inspected it. "Okay, I'm getting them."

Yay! Lilly squealed, as I tossed them in the basket, before moving on. Just as I turned to head for the next aisle, the hairs on the back of my neck stood on end as if I were being watched. *You're being paranoid. No one is watching you.* "How would you know?" *Don't worry about it. Why don't we go grab the dishes?*

"Alright," I nodded, pushing the nagging feeling aside as I strolled toward the kitchenware aisle. The shelves were packed with colorful supplies. Shiny pots and pans shimmered like trophies. *I want the purple ones. They're the cutest. And throw in some wine glasses.*

With a huff, I started sifting through the shelves, my fingers gliding over different textures.

Finally, I spotted the purple set tucked away in a corner, its glossy surface shimmering under the lights. A tag advertised its "vibrant glaze," and I smiled, recalling lavender fields swaying in the breeze. "How do you notice these things?"

It's a gift. I rolled my eyes before tossing the purple set, along with some wine glasses and a new coffee pot, into my basket. At the register, I shuffled into line, and a few customers cast curious glances my way.

Gee, there are some weirdos here. "No kidding," I whispered, fighting the urge to recoil under their scrutiny. "Next, please," the clerk called. I stepped forward, placing my items on the conveyor belt. As I rummaged through my purse for my wallet, the cashier—a young man with pale blond hair and striking blue eyes—sparked a flicker of warmth within me.

"Is there anything else I can help you with?" He leaned a bit closer, his gaze lingering. I met his eyes. "No thanks," I mumbled, noting how he shifted focus, almost as if gathering courage. "You moved into the cabin, right?" Surprised, I answered. "Yeah. How did you know?"

"Small town. Not much to do except listen to gossip," he said, a nervous laugh escaping his lips. I studied him closely, sensing the unease hidden behind his casual demeanor. "Aren't you scared of living there alone?" he asked, a hint of concern creeping into his voice.

I hesitated, momentarily caught off guard by his question. "No? Should I be?" He shook his head, but his gaze flickered away, betraying more than his words. "It's just...I've heard rumors about that place. The last owner was said to be a witch. Folks say she cursed it before she was brutally murdered during the witch trials."

I blinked. "A witch? What are you talking about?" He shrugged. "Well, I'm not really sure. Only that they had messed with the wrong woman.

Ever since then, that place has been cursed. Or so the legend goes." A laugh escaped me before I could stop it, even as the hair on my arms stood on end. "That's absurd. It's a regular cabin." He smirked, shaking his head. "You're probably right," his tone took on a casual air of nonchalance. "Anyway, welcome to Weathersfield. That'll be $32.47."

I dug through my purse, fishing out bills from my wallet as my hand trembled slightly. "Thanks, have a nice day," I offered a curt nod as I turned to leave. "Do you know anything about what he said?" I asked Lilly under my breath. *Nope, must be the work of the rumor mill.* I couldn't shake the tightness in my gut. "something's not right about that story." *You're being paranoid, again. It's just a stupid rumor.*

"If you know anything about that story, you need to tell me. It could be important." Her hesitation only unsettled me further. *Maybe I do, but you don't need to worry yourself over it.* "What do you mean, I shouldn't worry?" *I mean, you have no cause for concern, because I said so.* "That's not an answer." Silence stretched between us again as I made my way through the parking lot. "Dammit, Lilly, tell me."

Nothing. "Fine, forget it." I growled, shoving the grocery bags into the truck, locking the door. I needed a distraction, something to pull me away from the thoughts that were piling up. Leaning back against the truck, I glanced at a brochure I'd picked up while shopping. "Well, the Wethersfield Heritage Walk sounds interesting." *Everything sounds interesting to you,* Lilly quipped, a sarcastic edge to her voice. *But fine, I'm game. Let's take a walk through history, shall we, Em?* With a heavy sigh, I started my stroll down Main Street. The charm of the town surprised me. Each storefront burst with bright colors and quirky signs.

The Main Street Creamery & Cafe caught my eye with its deep purple wooden exterior, the scent of freshly baked pastries wafting from within. *You should try their lavender scones. They are to die for.* "Yeah, yeah," I muttered, even though the thought of a warm, buttery treat remained in my mind.

A girl needs to eat after all, right? As I turned a corner, the door swung open, and a man nearly knocked me over, his arms full of bouquets. I gasped, jumping back. "Sorry, excuse me." his eyebrows raised in surprise. "It's alright," I managed as he nodded and hurried away. I stared after him, my heart racing slightly from the encounter.

Shaking it off, I ordered a lavender scone and an iced coffee. Taking a sip, I nearly moaned as the flavor exploded on my tongue. *See, I told ya.* "It's not bad," I admitted, grinning.

With half a scone and my coffee in hand, I continued down the vibrant street. Following the blue signs guiding the Heritage Walk. Next up was The Cove, where the river met the shoreline.

As I approached, the gentle sound of water lapping against the banks greeted me. I paused at an exhibit kiosk detailing the historical significance of the area as birds flew overhead. *Legend has it that this was once a meeting spot for townsfolk and, well, something else. You know, when they still believed in witches and curses.*

I raised an eyebrow, taking a sip of my coffee. "It seems like they still believe. But what else do you know?" I asked, stepping closer to the bank. *I know plenty. This town has more secrets than people realize.* "Well, that's vague." A slow smile crept on my face. I rounded a corner, making my way to Broad Street, where families enjoyed the warmth of the day.

Kids chased each other, their laughter ringing out like music while others lounged on picnic blankets.

I stopped at another nearby kiosk, reading about the area's history. *Beautiful, isn't it? I spent many afternoons here, watching people come and go. Some say that when the sun sets, you can catch glimpses of those who lingered a bit too long during the trials.*

"Your fascination with the witch trials is borderline ridiculous, you know," I chuckled, shaking my head. *They're fascinating,* she retorted. I could almost feel her indignation radiating. "It's kind of creepy," I replied, deciding it was time to head home. As I made my way back to the truck, the sun dipped lower in the sky, casting long shadows across the quaint town.

My mind drifted, entertaining Lilly's stories of witches and the cashier's warning of curses while I sipped the remnants of my iced coffee. I muttered, shaking my head in disbelief. *You're losing it, Em. There's nothing to be afraid of.* I turned up the radio, tuning everything out and letting the music wash over me, drowning out my thoughts.

I watched the trees roll by in a blur, but then something darted from the side of the road, catching my attention. Out of nowhere, I saw another flash of movement—a figure stepping forward, too close to the asphalt, seemingly unaware of the truck racing toward them. *Em, watch out!* Lilly shouted. I slammed on the brakes, tires screeching against the road as my pulse thundered in my ears.

The truck jerked, skidding a few feet before coming to a halt. I looked around, frantic. But the figure was gone. I closed my eyes, pressing my forehead to the steering wheel while taking a few calming breaths before shifting into gear again. "If that was your doing, Lil. I'm going to perform an exorcism."

For a moment, I hesitated, unsure whether to continue or stay put. My nerves were frayed and my hands trembled slightly as I shook my head. "What was that?" I wondered aloud as I shifted gears.

Maybe that story you heard got to you more than you'd care to admit, she replied. *You need to be more careful. Sudden stops like that are dangerous. We're not in some fairy tale, Em.*

I was surprised that she actually sounded worried for once as I continued driving slowly through the twists and turns of the road. It wasn't until I pulled into the gravel drive that I felt a moment of complete dread settle over me. A shadow slipped past the kitchen window.

My heart thundered as I blinked several times, trying to rationalize what I witnessed. "Did you see that? I think someone's inside." *Maybe something's there, or maybe it's not.* "Very funny. But I'm serious," I hissed, opening the truck door. Grabbing the bags, I approached, my steps pausing at the threshold as I surveyed the property.

Everything appeared unchanged, the weeds overtaking the walkways exactly as I had left them. *Are you planning on going in or just standing there all day?* Lilly prodded. "Shut up," I snapped, heat rising to my face. Summoning every ounce of courage, I twisted the doorknob and stepped inside. Dim lighting cast eerie shadows across the room, heightening my senses as I stood frozen, straining to hear any hint of movement.

Ever consider you're overreacting? "Yeah, I don't think so." I closed the door behind me, the thud echoing in the silence. I took a cautious step forward, flicking on the lights. Carefully, I crossed the living room as the floor creaked, groaning beneath me as if protesting my intrusion.

I searched for any signs of life, but silence enveloped the room. *See? Nothing,* Lilly mocked lightly. I leaned against the fireplace, wrestling with doubt as exhaustion seeped in. "Alright. You win. There's nothing here." I muttered, relieved yet still on edge as I retreated to the kitchen.

I placed the bags on the table when Lilly's snickering echoed in my mind. "What are you up to?" I narrowed my eyes moments before a crinkled paper caught my attention. I reached down to find a note lying on the countertop. 'If you need a friend, feel free to call or text. P.S., be careful in that cabin of yours. — Alex. 555-626-9970.' I frowned, my mind racing. Did this fall out of the bag?

Why would the cashier be concerned about me? *Maybe he likes you.* "Don't be ridiculous. I just met him." *True. But I suppose it doesn't matter either way.* "What's that supposed to mean?" Another laugh escaped her, sending a chill coursing through me. *Whatever you want it to mean.* With a resigned sigh, I stared down at the note, contemplating whether to toss it aside or tuck it away.

Part of me hesitated, reluctant to lose the chance of having someone in town to talk to, even if it was a simple connection. Then, Lilly's voice cut through my thoughts again, taking on a serious tone: *There's something here, in this room.* My heart stopped in my chest as I pivoted, scanning the kitchen like a deer caught in headlights. "What is it? I don't see anything."

Keep looking. Cautiously, I approached the refrigerator, peering inside for a hidden creature lurking among the milk and leftovers. I scrutinized each item, but nothing seemed out of the ordinary—jars and bottles were in their typical spots. *No, not in the refrigerator you ditz, In the cabinet, the one under the sink.*

I hesitated for a brief moment before my gaze darted toward the cupboard under the sink. And with a yank, I flung the door open, half-expecting something to leap out at me. That's when I saw them—two golden orbs glimmering in the dim light. I choked back a gasp, stumbling back a step, blood rushing in my ears.

"What the hell, Lilly?" I looked down again, half-expecting to find a cat curled up in the shadows, but the cabinet space was now empty—save for a few cleaning supplies and an old sponge sat there, mocking me. *Oh, man. I got you good!* Lilly's laughter rang through the kitchen, enveloping me, but it did little to ease the shock.

I shook my head, glancing again toward the cabinet as my heart beat frantically. "Very funny. You almost gave me a heart attack." *Oh, come on. It was hilarious.* "Why do you do this to me?" I grumbled, slamming the cupboard door closed. I shot her a pointed look, trudging into the living room, where something odd caught my attention.

Frowning, I leaned in closer. An old newspaper lay there. Curiosity surged through me as I reached over and picked it up. The headline jumped out at me. "Townsfolk Vanishing—Witchcraft Suspected." "Typical small-town superstition," I muttered dismissively, rolling my eyes. "They'd blame anything strange on witchcraft back then."

Such arrogance, Lilly replied sharply. *They truly think their modern views are superior.* "Arrogance? That seems a bit extreme, don't you think?" I folded the newspaper, thinking about the weight of its history. *You say that, yet you've never lived in that era. You can't see how people perceive such things.* There was a gravity to her words that tugged at me.

I had grown up in the city, wrapped in the comforts of technology and progress. But deep down, I knew she was right. The past had a way of lingering. *You're stubborn,* she concluded. "And you're annoying," I shot back as I folded the newspaper, tucking it into the side table drawer.

"What's with all the witchcraft talk in this town?" I asked, flopping down on the sofa, grabbing the remote to turn on the TV. "Why does that topic bother you so much? Feeling some ancestral guilt?" Silence loomed heavy as I waited for some type of snarky response or comeback. "Oh, come on," I teased lightly, "I was only joking." But the stillness pressed against me. "Are you even real?" I challenged. *I've told you I am, even if it was a long time ago.*

"Then tell me, what happened here?" I pressed, resting my head against the soft throw pillow, fatigue settling in. More silence. I let out an exhausted sigh, closing my eyes. "Fine, keep your secrets. But eventually, you'll have to answer my questions." *We'll see,* she muttered as her voice faded into the shadows.

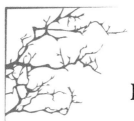

Hidden Threats

Footsteps echoed like a metal striking stone. I kept my voice sharp, but it wavered. "Lilly, if you're messing with me again, I'll scream loud enough to wake the dead." Silence was my only answer as I strained to pick up a laugh— a whisper. Anything to reveal she was just pranking me—but the hush was stifling. "Lilly..."

My throat ached, as if I had swallowed shards of glass. And still, there was no response. *Emma.* The way my name escaped her startled me. Light, yet ominous. Then, she was in front of me—looming and intense, like a wave crashing over me and sweeping everything else aside.

The air seemed dense, nearly suffocating, as though I was being dragged beneath the surface. Suddenly, it was as if the world around me dimmed, leaving only her presence in sharp focus. I could sense her energy crashing into me, a strange mix of exhilaration and dread, and I realized she was taking control.

Lilly

The urge to seize control surged, sharp and urgent. I have to do this now. No matter how much she kicked or screamed. I had commandeered her body only a handful of times before, each instance feeling like squeezing into clothes three sizes too small. How the hell did that damning newspaper get there? I'd been so careful. *Lilly? What the hell? Where am I?*

Her frantic voice echoed in my mind as her panic flooded in like a toxic fog. "Oh, don't worry Em. Everything's fine. I'm borrowing your body for a little test drive. Think of it as a spa day. You know, the kind where you're locked in a dark room."

Are you out of your mind? Let me out!

Let her out? The idea made me laugh. "Oh no, I think not.Think of me as your slightly psychotic roommate. I'll return everything eventually, I swear." Her resentment crashed into me like a storm, a heavy weight in my chest as I pushed her further back into her mental cage, effectively muffling her pathetic cries. She can't know, I thought as I shredded the damning newspaper into confetti.

Who left it here to begin with? Someone had to know my secret, but who? Hot fury coursed through me at the thought as I frantically searched for more evidence.

I'll find out who did this, and when I do. I'll make them suffer in ways they can't even imagine. I took a deep breath, regaining my composure as my gaze drifted around the room.

There were no other clues. Maybe it was simply an unfortunate coincidence, but something told me it wasn't. I turned and walked into the living room, flopping down on the couch. I grabbed the remote and clicked the TV on, desperate for a distraction from the creeping unease that accompanied the silence of the cabin.

While channel surfing, I stumbled upon a cheesy horror movie filled with terrible lines and exaggerated performances—the kind that was so bad it became unexpectedly hilarious. But soon, I began to notice an unsettling, foreboding presence. A shiver crept up my spine and the hairs on the back of my neck stood on end.

It was as if someone—or something—was watching me, lurking somewhere in the shadows. "Xander?" I called out hesitantly, my voice echoing back in the silence, but met only with emptiness. Xander sometimes wandered the property, waiting for the moment I took control, so we could spend time together. Shaking off the burst of apprehension, I got an overwhelming urge to escape the cabin.

I moved swiftly, changing into a tank top and a pair of shorts. Slipping on my sandals. With a calming breath, I stepped outside. The moment the door creaked shut, fresh air engulfed me, washing away the unease. With each step deeper into the woods, the coarse leaves crunched beneath my sandals, each sound a reminder that I was alive and free, at least for the moment.

Not having a determined destination, I let the trail lead me toward the pond a few miles away. Memories of its wicked past echoed in my mind. Of those who met horrible fates in these very woods, at the hands of fear and ignorance, binding them. Yet, despite the history, I felt a strange connection to this place, a fondness born from the very darkness that overshadowed it. After twenty minutes of wandering,

I finally arrived at the pond's edge, dipping my legs into the cool water. Ripples glided out, the refreshing touch enticing me to savor this moment. Soon, everything would change. And my existence would take on a new form. But as the peaceful moment faded, reality crept back in, and I knew it was time to return. To relinquish control back to Emma. Just as I began to prepare myself for the task, I opened my eyes—and froze.

Across the pond stood a man draped in a flowing crimson robe, his features obscured by the heavy fabric that swayed with the slightest breeze.

Magic rippled around him, wrapping itself around my senses. And my heart stuttered at the sight, but surprisingly, curiosity drowned out any hint of fear. A witch, perhaps? I hadn't encountered another witch since before my last demise, and his silent presence held an allure of powerful magic. Steeling myself, I carefully took a step backwards. As I turned to leave, a twig snapped under my foot, the sharp crack piercing the tranquil quiet.

I glanced back over my shoulder, only to find him moving silently, gliding effortlessly across the ground as he shadowed my steps."Okay, wise guy. Follow this," I muttered under my breath as I channeled my energy. I began humming my teleportation spell.

Then a flicker of magic ignited. I vanished from the edge of the pond in seconds, and reappeared in the familiar living room, landing on the wooden floor with a thud. "Okay, well. That was weird," I thought, trying to shake off the remnants of fear. I flopped back onto the couch. Feeling my heart still racing, a mix of confusion and curiosity swirling within me. Pressing my palms against my eyes, I took a moment to ground myself.

With a deep breath, I released my hold on control, letting Emma flood back in as I surrendered to the moment.

Emma

The cabin tilted and swayed as my vision blurred. Where am I? I called out, but the syrupy darkness swallowed my voice as a soft glow appeared. Beckoning through the haze like a lighthouse. I slogged forward, each step slow and agonizing. When I got closer, a candle came into focus. Behind it, an ivory-skinned woman with eyes of emerald green stood transfixed by the flame.

Delicate features belied an alluring, dangerous essence. I noticed her full lips and fathomless gaze as golden hair cascaded over her shoulders, trailing down her back and across her full breasts. Her voice was soft, whispering incantations into the shadows. Was this a memory? A dream? Had I blacked out?

I felt as if I were in a free fall, teetering on the edge of sanity. The woman before me was a mirror image of my imagination, down to the star-shaped birthmark that adorned her left wrist—exactly as I had visualized Lilly. Suddenly, the room ignited with a burst of bright light as she stood among the candlelight, eyes closed, chanting in a language I couldn't comprehend.

It was a sound that vibrated through my bones, resonant and haunting all at once. A man loomed behind her, his figure faint and ghostly, eyes locked onto her form as if she were the only thing that existed. Her words danced around me, the air humming with energy.

With each syllable she uttered, the cabin vanished like a mirage, replaced by an endless expanse of rolling hills and swaying grass. "Where the hell am I?" I gasped, but the words felt trapped, caught in my throat. And then, without warning, I drifted into a white haze, the world dissolving around me.

Until I found myself back on the couch in my cabin, reality crashing in like a cold wave. Lilly's voice echoed in my mind, a mocking laughter that surrounded me like a whirlwind. *There you are. I thought I'd lost you in the abyss this time.* "What in the actual hell happened?" I managed to choke out, my voice hoarse as I blinked against the dim light.

Nothing out of the ordinary. I think you must have just fallen asleep. "I didn't fall asleep, you psycho. What did you do to me?" *It must have been something you ate. Or imagined.* "You've got to be joking," I deadpanned. Somehow, I knew something crooked happened. But what?

I forced myself to sit up, ignoring the tilting, spinning world as my head throbbed. Nausea rose in my throat. "I need water." *Well, good luck with that.* Lilly's derisive chuckle was a stinging slap across the face.

I staggered towards the kitchen, my feet leaden as I gripped the countertop for support. My gaze fell on the faucet, and I grabbed a purple sparkly glass. Filling it to the brim. *Feel better?* "Much, no thanks to you." I shot back.

"Now, are you going to tell me what happened, or do I have to keep guessing?" She was silent, and I knew she was weighing her options. *No,*

27

but I do think it's time for bed. It's way too late to be up acting all crazy. Bed? I looked at the oven and the clock that somehow read 1:00 AM. How did it get so late?

Six hours have passed, unaccounted for. "Go to hell." I spat back, primal frustration overpowering my rationalization. *Already there, darlin'.* Her voice was matter-of-fact, without a hint of apology or remorse. With a frustrated growl, I grabbed my laptop from the coffee table and stalked off into my room. Still shaky, I flopped onto my mattress.

Think, what the hell happened? Why did she take over? Then, an idea struck me. I frantically typed in a search for witch trials in Weathersfield. As I sat before the glow of my screen, a Pandora's box of search results, the sinister history of the small town unfolded before me. Witch trials were commonplace during the 1600s and 1700s, and many people were unjustly persecuted, killed, and hung for their alleged crimes.

With trembling fingers, I scrolled past haunting images of accused witches, their lifeless bodies suspended from gnarled branches, or drowned within a pond. The vividness of the images were overwhelming. I could almost smell the smoke and taste the metallic tang of blood from those centuries-old pyres.

As I read through the articles, a name stopped me in my tracks. Lillith Carrington. However, before I could delve deeper into the story, the screen suddenly cracked, jolting me back to reality. "Lilly?" There was no response as my laptop shuddered on the bed as if struck by an invisible fist, its screen flashing white before abruptly winking out.

The pain that shot through my skull was excruciating. Causing me to let out a scream that barely escaped my lips. "Lilly. Enough!" The now-darkened laptop flew from my grip, landing with a heavy thud. Frustration and anger welled up. "What was that article going to reveal?" I shouted into the empty room, my voice filled with an urgent demand for answers.

"What are you hiding from me?" *You're just exhausted. Get some sleep.* Her words washed over me, draining the last vestiges of energy from my body, as if she had a magical hold on me. And soon, I slipped into unconsciousness.

Flashback

The smell of burning flesh and hair filled my nostrils, making my stomach churn with revulsion. The screams of a young girl pierced the air. Her red hair was a wild tangle, her limbs flailing wildly as she struggled to break free. The fire crackled and spat, sending sparks flying upwards into the overcast sky.

As I watched, a man dressed as a priest stepped forward, his eyes burning like the embers of the raging fire. He held a Bible in one hand, his other hand grasping a wooden cross. He began to chant, his voice rising above the cacophony of screams and flames. "You are a servant of Satan!" he shouted. "You have brought darkness and evil upon our village!

You must be purged!" The men holding the girl down tightened their grip, their faces set in cruel grins.

Flames danced higher, casting flickering shadows on the faces of the crowd. "No, no, no! You can't do this to me, please, stop!" She begged. Terror saturated her voice, as her eyes were wild and glossy. The men ignored her cries, dragging her further towards the towering fire.

Soon, they'll throw me on that pile of kindling, and when the fire is hot enough, my flesh will sizzle and pop as they laugh and taunt me. "You don't have to do this!" an elderly man pleaded, his eyes wide and desperate. "She's my daughter, not a witch! Please, I'll give you anything. Please, let her go!"

The guards paused, as if considering the man's broken pleas. But with a disgusted grunt, they tied the girl to the stake and lit it. Watching the flames lick at her heels with a sickening, gleeful expression. Her screams turned feral, like a wounded animal at slaughter mixing with the screams and cries of her father.

A sickly stench mingled with the smoke until I gagged. Eventually, her cries diminished to a gurgling rasp. My vision blurred when her father let out a wail mixed with sobs, his heart-rending cries sending a cold shudder down my spine. "My baby girl, my sweet girl," his voice was full of grief, so heavy it weighed upon me.

He resigned, as his soul was torn away, leaving merely a shell of a man behind. The burly men turned to me next. "I'll be back. And when I do, you'll be the first two I kill." I spat, "I'm going to bathe in your blood and laugh while I do it!" I put on my most vicious grin.

Their laughter answered my threat as they dragged me towards the next stake. I didn't struggle, it would be useless. Besides, my fate is sealed now. Closing my eyes, I began singing a low-tuned spell to numb the pain before they tied me up to burn. "The flames will rage, but I'll not go. Block the pain and let me flow." "You think that little tune of yours will work on us?" One laughed mockingly.

"It's not for you, idiot." I snapped. Then took a deep breath, forcing myself to ignore the approaching flames. The men watched with amusement as my body reacted, even though I couldn't feel the flames licking at my flesh. I hated them for making me watch myself die like this - melting, burning.

This town, these people, they're all going to pay. My last coherent thought was a promise of revenge. One I fully intended to fulfill.

Temptations Of Eternity

I sat motionless on the edge of the bed, my legs dangling over the side as I stared blankly at the pale walls that seemed to close in on me. The memories of last night's vivid dream clung to me like sticky cobwebs—it seemed too real to shake off. I still heard the echo of screams fading into silence and a knot twisted in my stomach.

Glancing at the clock, I noted the hands ticking away the early morning hours—5:30 AM. Too early to be up, yet too late to sink back into the sweet oblivion of sleep. I let out a resigned sigh that tasted like defeat. Propping myself up, I pushed away the spiraling thoughts that threatened to pull me back down and shuffled toward the kitchen.

As I entered the kitchen, a familiar ritual responded to my arrival—the rich aroma of fresh coffee filled the air, swirling around me and wrapping me in its comforting embrace. It was a thin veil of normalcy amidst the disquiet that lingered like an unwelcome guest. I poured myself a steaming cup.

The heat prickled at my fingers, and took a sip, letting it spread through me. The morning news droned softly in the background, a tapestry of doom and despair that I'd rather not pay attention to.

Headlines of disappearances and unexplained deaths danced across the screen, each report more chilling than the last. *I may know something about that.* I flinched, her voice breaking me out of my spiraling thoughts. "Not now," I muttered. Too tired to deal with her.

But where's the fun in tha- Before she finished speaking, a loud knock echoed from the door. Startling, I nearly dropped my mug as I rushed towards the sound. *Oh goody, a visitor!* "Who is it?" I asked warily, my hand hovering over the handle. *It's him.*

Alex

I banged on the cabin door, my heart frantically pounding like a drum in my chest. "Emma! Open up!" I was on the verge of imploding. I had to warn her—she had to understand what was going on. This wasn't me being paranoid. No, this was real. My memory flashed back to when he took control. Standing in the woods, Emma's glee was evident.

But it wasn't Emma. No, he had called her...Lillith. When she finally cracked open the door, the confused look on her face had me thinking twice about what I should say, but there was no other option. "What the hell are you doing here?"

"Is anyone else here?" I blurted out, stepping inside without waiting for an invitation. I swept the room, my pulse racing in rhythm with my thoughts. "I heard you talking to someone." Her confusion deepened, and that put me on edge. "What are you talking about? There's no one here," she replied, and my grip on sanity began to fade away. "You don't understand. This place is cursed." I said, lowering my voice to a whisper, searching her eyes for understanding.

"The whole town is—you have to believe me." I needed her to see, to feel the urgency of my words. When she stepped back, the panic inside me boiled up into something raw. "The witch who owned this cabin put a curse on it. I came here to protect you!"

I was spiraling, there was no doubt about it, but I had to make her understand. "Enough," she snapped at me, her tone sharp enough to slice through the chaos in my mind. "Stop. There's no one here besides us. Please leave." Her wide blue eyes caught mine, and I felt a surge of desperation. "I'm trying to help."

It felt like the walls were closing in, and I needed her to know I wasn't losing it. My thoughts tumbled over one another in a race of chaos. What if Lillith was in her head already? What if she was pulling the strings? The thought made me nauseous.

"Please, listen to me." I pleaded. "Thanks, but I'm fine," she replied with forced calmness, pushing me toward the door as if I were a pesky fly. "Wait! Remember what I said." I called out, feeling the door rattle shut behind me. I turned and pressed my forehead against the cool wood. That didn't go as planned at all.

"Let it go, Alex. She's fine. You're being foolish," came a voice deep within my mind. One that slithered into my psyche. I knew he held a connection to Emma, somehow, and that connection made my skin crawl.

Emma

I leaned back against the door, trying to steady myself as my head throbbing. I couldn't take much more of this. This town is crazy. Bat shit insane, and somehow, I'd landed right in the middle of the crazy conspiracies. I had a strong urge to get the hell out of the town and never look back, but of course.

It would be wrong to waste the gift my parents gave me. Especially over some nonsense. My stomach was twisting itself into knots. *Just relax, Em. He's a loon. A cute, charming loon, but still. All the same.* I shook my head, ignoring Lilly's dismissal. A part of me felt guilty for blowing him off, but what could I do?

He was obviously not in his right mind. And the last thing I needed was to get involved with a delusional stalker. It was bad enough that Lilly was already in my head. And yet, a small part of me couldn't help but wonder if there was any truth to his story.

The shadow that passed by the window. Was it one of Lilly's tricks, or something more tangible? And if so, how was anyone else able to see it? I tried not to think about it. But it nagged at me like a pesky fly buzzing around my head. "Is there something you're not telling me?"

Silence greeted my question. "Answer me." Still no response. With a groan, I grabbed a pen, determined to write down every weird little detail, no matter how crazy it sounded. "If you won't tell me what's going on. Then I'll have to figure it out for myself," I muttered under my breath, the pen scribbling furiously across the page.

The more I wrote, the clearer things became. "Alex wasn't lying, was he?" My heart skipped a beat as realization dawned on me. Something wasn't adding up, and the truth was becoming stranger than fiction. "Lilly, are you the witch who lived in this cabin?"

My words were barely a whisper, but they echoed in the empty space, filling the air with an unspoken question. "If you won't talk, then I'll keep digging," I threatened. "And I won't stop until I get some answers." Just then, a cold draft filled the cabin, the chill sending a shiver through me. The curtains fluttered, and I felt her presence lingering beyond reach. Somehow, I knew she was listening.

Even if she wasn't speaking. With a resigned sigh, I turned off the lights and walked to my room. With the door closing behind me, and darkness engulfing the space.

Dream

The soft caress of Xander's fingers trailed down my arm, sending shivers across my skin as his brilliant green eyes roamed over me, devouring every curve. The golden light of the setting sun filtered through the thick leaves of our tree beside the pond. Its gnarled branches provided a sense of shelter and intimacy.

"You're stunning, Lillith. Truly," he murmured, his voice warm and honeyed. I could feel the heat of the earth within the soil beneath my feet. Making the moment feel timeless. "Do you promise this will work?" I asked, my voice barely above a whisper. Doubt gnawed at the edges of my mind like the ripples that shimmered across the pond's surface.

"I promise," he replied, pressing a soft kiss on my neck, his breath tickling my ear and sending an electric jolt through me."Everything will be perfect." Closing my eyes, I savored the feeling. His closeness, the smell of cedar, and sunlight that caught in his hair.

I bit my lip, doubt still lingering in the back of my mind as my fingers danced up his chest, reveling in the sharp intake of his breath that told me my touch ignited him."I never imagined being able to spend endless lifetimes with you," he whispered, his voice husky.

The very idea had both excitement and uncertainty swirling in my stomach. "Each generation will only make our love stronger. Imagine what we could become in a few centuries." His words settled around me, and my smile faded like the sun dipping below the horizon. "I'm not sure that's something we should be proud of," I said quietly, my gaze dropping to the water.

"Oh, come on, Lil," he crooned, gently tilting my chin up, forcing me to meet the intensity of his gaze. His hand trailed down to my hip, fingers tracing patterns on my skin, and igniting a warmth that spread like wildfire through my veins.

"Don't you want to live forever? To get revenge?" I shook my head, unable to tear my gaze away from his. "I want to be with you. I don't care about any of that. I would give anything to stay with you. That's all I've ever wanted." The truth in my voice surprised me, but it resonated deep within my heart.

His expression softened, eyes glimmering under the growing night. He took my hand, interlacing our fingers. "Even after a thousand years, I'll find you," he promised, his voice low and steady, like the heartbeat of the earth beneath us. "I'll be with you, to hold your hand through it all."

My eyes flickered over him as his promise sank in, the weight of eternity making my head spin. Forever. "Promise?"

His smile was more dazzling than the stars above. "Always." I didn't need to hear anything else. The connection between us held the depth of the universe. He closed the distance, bringing his lips to mine in a tender kiss.

It was a blend of everything we were and what we could become.

As he pulled away, a chorus of crickets began to serenade the deepening night. "Let's make this the first of many moments."

Emma

I woke with a start, the vivid memory of Xander's promise ringing in my ears. Lilly has to be this Lillith I keep dreaming of. But why is she in my head? What does she want? And who was Xander? My head was spinning with unanswered questions as I glanced at the clock, noting the time. 10:00 am.

Great, I overslept. With a groan, I scrambled out of bed, my feet hitting the cool floor with a muted thud. The sun peeked timidly through the curtains, casting a hazy glow across the room, but Lilly was still asleep. I had hoped anyway.

I glanced around, half-expecting her to leap out from the shadows.

Determined to start the day on my terms, I hurried to the kitchen. I pictured the rich scent of freshly brewed coffee, a quick bite to eat, and then I'd be out the door. Armed with whatever chaos awaited. But as I looked around the kitchen, my stomach dropped.

I was fresh out of my morning coffee. "Crap," I muttered, letting out a frustrated breath as I surveyed the pile of dishes coated in last night's grime, the remnants of our half-eaten dinner still staring back at me. I realized there was no time for coffee or food.

Instead, I grabbed my bag. The straps biting into my shoulder as I flung it over my back. Each step out the door felt like a race against time. The Library had to be open by now, and if I could reach it before Lilly stirred from her slumber, I might find the answers I desperately needed.

As I slammed the door shut behind me, the cool morning air rushed against my skin, waking me up out of my morning haze. I quickened my pace, the sound of my sneakers crunching against the gavel and echoing in my ears. Each beat of my heart echoed a silent countdown, a push to get to the Library before the day—and Lilly—could catch up with me.

My truck sputtered and coughed, the engine struggling to turn over. But after a few minutes, it finally roared to life, and I sighed in relief. The drive into town seemed shorter than usual, and I found myself pulling up to the Library in record time.

I parked the truck, heading inside, and hoping to find someone who could point me in the right direction. The library shelves were scant, and I couldn't find much information on any of the town's history, other than a few newspaper clippings and dusty old books.

"Excuse me, ma'am, can I help you?" I spun around, nearly jumping out of my skin at the sudden intrusion. "Yes, actually. I'm looking for some information on the town."

The librarian looked surprised momentarily before speaking. "Wait, aren't you the new owner of that cabin? On the northern edge of town?"

"Yeah. Why do you ask?" I responded, glancing around the dusty shelves. "That cabin has stories," she said, narrowing her eyes thoughtfully at me. "Weathersfield is steeped in history, but not the good kind. The tales date back hundreds of years—curses, hauntings, mysterious disappearances, and even unexplained deaths."

"And did you know this town was crucial during the witch trials?" I swallowed hard, trying to maintain my composure. "Witch trials?" I echoed, unsure where this conversation was heading.

"Absolutely. In the late 1600s, hysteria swept through New England like wildfire. In 1672, several women were tried here—innocent scapegoats caught in society's fears. Many were hanged, others faced far worse fates at the stake. It was a dark time, filled with paranoia, and the echoes of that fear linger still."

"Surely, that's old folklore, right? Exaggerations over time?" I stammered, feeling dread creep into my bones. "Maybe," she replied, skepticism lacing her tone. "But look around. This town's population is low for a reason. People tend to leave as soon as possible." What have I gotten myself into? My mind raced with thoughts of Alex's warnings. This town is insane. Maybe it really was time to escape Weathersfield.

After the librarian finished her tirade of doom and gloom, I quickly thanked her and exited the building. I climbed into the truck and headed to the closest gas station. My truck wasn't going to make it much further without a little help. While filling the tank, I noticed a local shop selling tourist trinkets and such.

On a whim, I wandered inside, thinking a souvenir might bring a little comfort. A bell jingled, announcing my arrival. "Hello, dearie. What can I help you with?"

A kind voice came from behind the counter, where an older woman settled amid towering stacks of books and trinkets. She adjusted her glasses, peering at me with bright blue eyes that sparkled with curiosity and warmth.

Her silver hair loosely pinned up in a bun, stray wisps framing her face like soft clouds. "Just looking around, thanks," I replied, forcing a smile that felt a bit too tight. I stepped past her. The creaking floorboards beneath my feet shifted slightly.

As I wandered through the labyrinth of tables and furniture, the scent of aged paper and polished wood surrounded me. Dust motes danced slowly in the streams of sunlight that filtered through a grand, stained-glass window, the colors basking the room in a warm glow. I ran my fingers along the spines of the books, feeling the textured bindings beneath my touch.

It was then, among the flickering shadows, I stopped abruptly, my breath hitching in my throat. An antique picture frame hung askew on the wall, drawing me in like a magnet. The frame was ornate, gilded edges glinting in the soft light, but it was the photograph within that stole my breath. My heart stuttered as I recognized her face—Lilly, unmistakable in her youth, her smile illuminating the sepia-toned image.

She stood beside a man whose presence seemed to radiate an energy all his own. His jet-black hair fell in smooth waves around his sharp features, glinting like obsidian, while his piercing forest green eyes seemed to hold the secrets of the world, intense and enigmatic. He seemed familiar. Like a far-off dream I couldn't quite grasp. I stepped closer, my breath shallow, and my pulse a frantic rhythm in my ears. Time seemed to slow as my eyes roamed over the photo, drinking in the details. The man's cheekbones were prominent, enough to cut glass, and the way he leaned toward Lilly carried an air of intimacy that sent an inexplicable chill down my spine.

Turning the frame gingerly, I flipped it over, revealing the date scrawled hastily in the corner: 1672. A wave of disbelief washed over me, mingling with the fervent curiosity igniting my thoughts. How had Lilly ended up here? "What can you tell me about this?" I asked, my finger lightly tracing the edge of the ornate frame as I pointed to the photograph.

The woman's expression shifted, a mixture of nostalgia and caution flickering across her features. "Oh, that was a young couple, infamous for being the highlight of the Wethersfield witch trials," she replied, her voice taking on a conspiratorial tone. "Both tried and executed at the stake. It was then auctioned off from the original Carrington estate. A piece of history, it is. Are you a history buff?"

I nodded, though the term "buff" felt too strong for my scattered knowledge. "Something like that," I admitted, my mind still reeling. "Do you have anything else like this?" I asked, hopefully. "Afraid not," she sighed. "This piece is one of a kind. But I have lots of other lovely things."

She gestured around the shop, her hands sweeping through the air as if conducting an orchestra. "I'm sure," I muttered, the spark of curiosity extinguished. With a polite nod, I turned to leave, a vague sense of disappointment pooling in my chest.

"Have a lovely day," she called out as the door creaked shut behind me. The bright afternoon sun hit me as I stepped outside, momentarily lifting my spirits. I decided to make a quick stop at the gas station on my way home.

Partially to shake off the unsettling weight of the day's discoveries. The bell above the door jingled as I entered, and the cool air, tinged with the scent of gasoline and roller snacks, enveloped me.

I grabbed a soda and a beef jerky stick, my fingers brushing against the cool cans as I tossed them onto the counter.

The cashier—a young guy with a crooked smile—ringing up my items gave me a nod as I paid. The sporadic sound of the register chimed against the backdrop of muffled conversation.

With my treasures in hand, I headed outside, the sun sinking lower in the sky, casting long shadows across the asphalt as I made my way to my truck. As I slipped into the driver's seat, I couldn't help but replay the conversation in my head, the photograph vivid in my memory.

I turned on the engine, and the radio cracked to life, but as I drove, the signal grew weak, fading in and out. I fumbled with the dial, twisting and turning it in a futile attempt to find a clearer channel. The radio fizzled once again, drowning my thoughts in a white noise that felt more suffocating than soothing.

With a resigned sigh, I switched the radio off, rolling down the window instead. The wind rushed in, tousling my hair and filling the car with a wild, free-spirited scent.

I could feel the sun's warmth against my skin. Yet, as I pulled into the familiar gravel driveway of my cabin, a chilling sense of dread coiled around my insides.

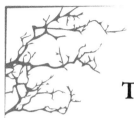

The Witch's Host

My thoughts spun as I sat on the old, worn couch, staring at the wooden coffee table in front of me. The flickering flames in the fireplace cast a warm glow, but I was anything but cozy. My mind was racing. I only hoped that this plan would work. My eyes drifted to the clock on the mantle, the slow tick seeming to echo throughout the house.

Time was running out. My stomach twisted as I thought about what could happen if he took control again, if I failed. Emma was going to be pissed and probably scared.

After all, I had climbed through her window like some kind of nightmare stalker. My fingers drummed impatiently against the worn fabric of the couch I had camped out on—its upholstery rough beneath my fingertips. Come on, hurry up. The thick, musty smell of old books and a hint of lavender hung in the air, mixing with my growing anxiety. I glanced around the dimly lit room, as I listened intently for any sign that Lillith was lurking. Finally, the sound of a lock clicking open pierced the silence, and my heart skipped a beat.

The front door creaked slowly, revealing Emma standing there, eyes wide with fear. My pulse quickened at the sight of her, but judging by the look on her face, she wasn't happy to see me. "What the hell are you doing here?" She let out a yelp as she stumbled back, nearly tripping over the threshold.

I could see her pulse pounding through the vein on her neck, her cheeks flushed crimson. Her dark, curly hair was tousled, giving her an endearing look that clashed dramatically with her annoyed expression. The flickering light from the hallway cast long shadows across her face, illuminating the mixed emotions swirling in her eyes as they darted between me and the open door behind her.

Swiftly, I moved in between her and the door, the cool wood pressing against my back as I closed it. "I'm sorry. But I need you to listen to me. We're running out of time, Emma." Her eyes widened, looking like a caged animal caught in a beam of light, desperately searching for an escape.

I could see her pulse quickening, each heartbeat echoing my own rising panic. The walls of her living room seemed to close in around us. But this time, to my surprise, she didn't yell. Didn't freak out. She stood there, trembling slightly, her breath hitching in her throat as she processed my words.

The normally easy-going spark in her eyes dimmed into a stormy haze of fear and the sight twisted something deep within me. I hated seeing her like this—hated even more that I had caused it. "I'm sorry for barging in like this. But both of our lives are in danger the longer w—" I began, but then the words crumbled in my mouth.

"No, not again." My tongue felt leaden, as if it were dragging through thick molasses. Fear curled around my stomach like a vice, squeezing tighter, colder, making it hard to breathe. The room tilted slightly, and an overwhelming sense of dread washed over me as those familiar, icy tendrils of panic crept in.

A dull throb began in my temples, accompanied by the familiar presence that pressed against my mind like a heavy weight. I recognized that force all too well—the creeping sensation that tightened around my thoughts like a shackle, reminding me that I was not entirely in control.

Emma

"I'm sorry for barging in like this. But both of our lives are in danger the longer w-" His words faltered, eyes glazing over. I stepped forward, kneeling beside him, even as fear threatened to spill over. "Hey, are you okay?" He nodded before he attempted to speak again, but his entire demeanor shifted. Instinctively, I took a step back.

The air seemed to change as a shiver ran down my spine. I could see his eyes darkening, going from an innocent, concerned gaze to something of a predator. Okay, this is getting weird. "I apologize. I was overwhelmed." He looked up at me, eyes somehow more intense than before. "But I know how we can fix this.

How we can get rid of Lilly for you." How does he know about her? A cold draft passed through the room, sending a shiver down my spine.

"How would you know anything about Lilly?" I asked, my voice wavering slightly. "I was raised in this town. I've seen a lot of terrible things. And I've dedicated myself to stop her. She's out to kill you." Kill me? My heart was racing as my mind struggled to process what he was saying. "Why would she want to kill me?

I haven't done anything to her," I asked, the words slipping out before I could stop them. My gut twisted into knots as Alex simply stared at me, his expression inscrutable, but I could sense a wave of emotions lurking beneath the surface, ready to spill over. "She wants to take over your body permanently," he finally replied, his voice low and slow.

The words hit me like a punch to the stomach, knocking the wind out of me. My mind reeled, spinning like a dizzy top.

I had suspected for a while that Lilly had an agenda—her possessiveness was a constant thorn in my side—but killing me?

This was an entirely different beast. "If what you're saying is true, why are you helping me? How can you even stop her?" I pressed, the tremor in my voice betraying my growing anxiety. All those playful encounters, the light teasing, they whirled around in my memory like leaves caught in a sudden gust.

Had I missed the signs all along? Alex's face hardened, the softness vanishing as quickly as it came. "You wouldn't be the first person she's done this to. And I'll be damned if I let her hurt another soul. She has to be stopped." His voice cut through the suspense, uncompromising. I met his gaze, and in that moment, I saw a blend of determination and fear swimming in those depths—an emotion I couldn't shake from my mind, even if I wanted to.

"I have a plan, but we have to act fast, because we don't have much time." I took a moment, overwhelmed, my inner turmoil writhing like a hurricane. I didn't want to trust him—not after everything that had happened. But Lilly's lies and coyness echoed in my mind, haunting whispers threading through my thoughts.

She was hiding something deeper and darker than I'd ever imagined. And if Alex was right, I had to stop her before it was too late. "What's your plan?" My voice was steadier now, but the flutter of doubt still danced in my stomach as I caught a flicker of a smirk creeping across his lips, a devil-may-care grin that only sent another shiver coursing through me.

"There's a ritual we can do. It will send her soul into the afterlife. Where it belongs. You'll have your life back. And you'll be safe." The thought of the afterlife hung in the air—a tantalizing vision, but like a mirage, it seemed far out of reach.

I swallowed hard, weighing the odds. "You're sure this will work?" My voice was small, almost lost among the shadows gathering in my mind. His expression turned serious, grounding me in the gravity of the situation. "I'm positive. If we do this right, she won't ever be able to hurt you again."

Inside, a war waged. I glanced toward the window. The dim light filtering through the curtains seemed to darken, mirroring my thoughts.

Was I ready to trust Alex, of all people, with my safety? I swallowed the lump in my throat. "Okay, I'm in. What do we have to do?" His expression softened as he took a step closer.

I could smell his cologne. Spicy and woodsy, like the rest of him. "We'll need some things, salt, candles, and a few other ingredients. And we have to go to the original site of her death."

The original site of her death. I didn't even know where Lilly came from. "Where is that?" His eyes locked with mine, his expression intense. "It's by a pond on the outskirts of town. Where they drowned, hung, or burned accused witches." My stomach dropped as the pieces fell into place.

I should have known from the first nightmare I had of her being burned. But a part of me didn't want to accept that Lilly was a witch. I looked up at him, my eyes pleading. "We have to do this tonight. Please, I can't live like this anymore." He nodded. "I understand. Tonight, we'll end this. If you have any candles, grab them. I'll drive us to the site."

His words were comforting. Knowing I wasn't alone in this, and having a solid plan, eased my anxiety. At least, a little. "Okay, I'll pack a bag. Do we have to worry about anything else?" "Not unless Lilly takes control of you. Then she'll try to stop it." He glanced around the room.

"She could be listening. Grab a few candles, and we'll figure it out from there."

I nodded, grabbing a couple of candles from the kitchen counter and stuffing them in my backpack as Alex watched me intently. I felt his eyes on me as I moved around the house, and I couldn't help but notice the way the light from the fire danced across his features. He was beautiful. I'd admit to that. But, right now, I have more pressing matters.

With my backpack slung over my shoulder, I followed him outside. He led the way to a silver pickup truck parked alongside a dirt road a little way from my house. I climbed in, and he started the engine. As the truck pulled out of the driveway, a twinge of doubt lingered. Did I really trust him?

He had broken into my house after all, and now he was dragging me out to some unknown location in the middle of the night. And he had knowledge about Lilly that he shouldn't. Yet, a small voice inside my head whispered, if he was lying, what did I have to lose? "Emma?" His voice startled me. I realized he's waiting for me to answer... something. "Oh, um sorry. What did you say?"

"I was asking if you're okay? You seem on edge," he asked, concern etched in his voice. "I'm fine," I replied, forcing a smile. "It's just that, this whole thing sounds like a really bad horror movie," I grumbled. He snickered, his eyes fixed on the road ahead.

He didn't seem like a serial killer, and he didn't seem like he was leading me to my doom. So, at least there was that. The headlights illuminated the empty highway as we drove deeper into the forest. The trees loomed tall and dark around us, casting eerie shadows in the moonlight. I had to force myself to relax, reminding myself that I was safe—for now.

As we drove, the scenery shifted from the familiar chaos of town to a more sedate setting. A clearing blossomed before us, framed by towering evergreens.

A small pond shimmered in the distance, its surface reflecting the moonlight like a liquid mirror.

Fields stretched out, grass glistening under the silvery light, and then there was a small log cabin, nestled beside the trees. It looked as if it had been abandoned for years, with creeping vines and weathered wood. "This is it," Alex said, his voice hushed, pulling me from my daze. The air was thick with the sounds of crickets serenading the night.

"Where do we perform the ritual?" I asked, aiming to keep my voice steady. "The middle of the field," he replied, pointing toward the grassy expanse that stretched out. His tone was matter-of-fact, as if we were discussing the weather rather than preparing for something that might change my life.

"Here, let me get things set up." I watched as he moved with purpose, gathering stones and placing them in a perfect circle, a gathering of natural witnesses for the evening's events. With careful precision, he positioned a candle in the center—its wick standing tall, waiting to be lit.

The flicker of flame danced like a heartbeat in the stillness. "Are you sure this will work?" I found myself asking again as doubt swept through me. I mean, who really believes in all this stuff? "Without a doubt," he replied easily, and he shot me a reassuring smile.

I wanted to believe him, to trust that this was the path forward, yet seeds of uncertainty thrived in the corners of my mind. But in the end, even if it didn't work, what difference would it make? "Now, I'll need your blood," he continued, his tone turning serious, "and then I'll take care of the rest."

"My blood?" It took a moment for the gravity of his request to sink in, and suddenly, the reality of what we were about to do weighed heavily on my chest like lead.

"Yeah. Just a small cut on your finger and a few drops on the ground. I'll need to mix it with the herbs and candles, and we'll be all set."

"Okay," I said, steeling myself for the pain. As he produced a pocket knife, my hands began trembling again. In one swift motion, he sliced the tip of his finger.

Blood welled up in a dark red pebble that glistened against his skin, and he smeared it across the blade, "a symbol of the price we must pay for this ritual," he mumbled. With a deep breath, I extended my hand toward him, offering my palm like a sacrificial lamb to slaughter.

Without warning, He pressed the edge against my skin, and in a swift motion, a sharp sting—a jolt of pain that was momentary but fierce, shot through me. The sight of my blood, dark and vivid, made my stomach flip and my world slightly tilt.

He gathered the ingredients with a surprising calmness, each item adding to the unsettling mood of the night. Bits of dried herbs, a small vial filled with an iridescent liquid, and, of course, a drop of blood from his, and my finger. Glistening like tiny rubies in the dim light.

We mixed them together in an old, weathered bowl as he began uttering a chant so softly it was almost lost in the wind. The candle flickered wildly beside us, casting dancing shadows across the pond, making me feel like I was caught between realms. While illuminating his features. "Blood is a powerful ingredient." Despite the circumstances, his voice was steady. "It represents life, and by offering it, we're showing our willingness to make a sacrifice for greater good."

"Right," I muttered, feeling a knot form in my stomach as he moved closer, holding the bowl—a concoction that looked both sacred and sinister.

"Close your eyes." His tone softened, but there was a seriousness about it that made me comply without thinking. "I'll start the incantation. Just remember, whatever you do, don't open your eyes."

I nodded,and a moment later the air seemed to shift. As if it had decided to hold its breath. I could feel an energy swirling around us, raising the tiny hairs on my arms as if I were about to be electrocuted. His voice grew stronger as he recited the strange words, their rhythms rolling off his tongue easily.

His words echoed and pulsed through the energy as if they were physically affecting it. I tried to focus on the chant, but I couldn't help feeling that it was invoking something sinister. A buzzing noise began to grow in my ears. Humming in an odd crescendo. And suddenly, a sharp burst of pain slammed into me, like someone had driven a white-hot poker into my brain. My eyes flew open instinctively as I gasped. My vision was swallowed by darkness, and for a moment, it was as if time itself had stopped.

The Soul Taker's Lament

Emma

The pungent aroma of patchouli and herbs invaded my nose as I stood, frozen in a prison of flesh and bone. Lilly's lover's words reached my ears, and I looked up to find him staring at me. "You're everything to me. I can't let you go."

I was trapped, unable to move or speak as words poured out of me unbidden. "Do you think it will work? The curse, the spell, all of it?" The question hung in the air as he leaned in, eyes blazing with danger as his lips met mine.

The contact was electric, warm, soft, and passionate - yet tinged with a darkness that sent shivers skittering through me. I struggled to break free, writhing inwardly like a caged beast, but it was no use.

After a moment, he pulled away. His expression was one of pure ecstasy as he tilted my chin up, forcing me to meet his gaze. "It will work," he said as his thumb stroked my cheek. "You're my entire world. And my love for you has no bounds."

"I love you too." Despite my resistance, I professed, "I'd do anything for you." He smiled, his eyes shining with adoration. Somehow, I was helpless to stop what was happening.

"You're exquisite," he purred. "Let's celebrate the beginning of forever, together." He reached out for my hand, leading me to the bedroom. No, no, no...shit! My breath came in faster as he laid me on the bed. And I fought desperately to break free, clawing at the walls of my prison.

His hands roamed over my body, exploring every inch. The feeling was muted, but I sensed the pleasure, the intensity of it all still.

Suddenly, a tremendous crash echoed downstairs and angry shouts filled the space. "What's happening?" He pressed a finger to my lips. "Shhh. It'll be alright." Swiftly, he moved to the dresser, blocking the door. "Witch hunters." He looked back, a devilish smirk playing on his lips, as if the thought thrilled him to the core. My mind was racing. If they killed him, would I be stuck like this forever? What even is this?

I can't move, can't talk, can't control my actions. "What should we do?" The words tumbled out. "Grab the book. I'll lead them away from here. Once we're clear, I'll deal with them."

"Are you sure about this?" My voice quivered. "Yes. Go out the window, and I'll meet you at our spot." He pressed a quick kiss to my cheek, a fleeting warmth against the chill of the room, and then hurried out without another word.

The wood dresser scraped against the floor with a loud scrape before the door slammed behind him. Echoing in the chaos. My heart raced at the sudden urgency, knowing I had to follow orders and grab the book from the shelf.

My fingers brushed against the grainy, dust-coated surface as I scanned row after row of spines until I spotted the faded leather cover of the grimoire. Wedged in tightly between two other books—the perfect hiding spot. It took a little muscle to pry it free.

The book resisted, but soon, a puff of dust trailed in its wake. Securing it under my arm, I turned to the window. The frame was stiff, and for a moment, I strained against it, my heart in my throat as I struggled to shake it loose. Finally, with a bit of elbow grease, it swung open with a satisfying creak.

A breeze rushed in and tousled my hair as I clambered onto the ledge, the rough wood biting into the palms of my hands, for a second, I took a moment to breathe in the night.

The air outside was fresh and crisp, carrying with it a blend of earthy scents—a hint of pine from the nearby trees and the faintest trace of damp earth.

It was a stark contrast to the stale, candle-warmed air I had left behind. But that moment of peace shattered as the sounds of shouts echoed in the distance, sharp and urgent like a siren call beckoning forward.

With a surge of adrenaline, I leaped down, landing softly on the grass outside. With the forest surrounding me, shadows stretched and flickered beneath the sparse light of the moon. I sprinted forward, into the embrace of the trees, hearing a loud crack that sounded from behind me. My breath caught, and I froze in place. Was that a gun? Or something worse? The echoes of screams of agony soon followed it.

"What was that?" My pulse quickened as I ducked and weaved between the trees. Of course, I had no idea where I was going. But Lilly sure did. She maneuvered through the undergrowth like a deer, as the thrill of the chase flowed through her veins.

Her hair fluttered in the wind as we stumbled into a small clearing with a pond and a beautiful cabin. This must be 'their spot.' The realization hit me like a gut punch, and my heart dropped as the pieces fell into place. This was the place Alex took me to get 'rid' of Lilly. The truth crashed over me, icy and painfully obvious.

He lied to me—but why? Unable to contain the swirling chaos inside, a haunting tune began to spill from my lips, each note resonating with a strange, almost magnetic pull. "Devourer, devourer. Gather your power, for I will live for eternity. Devourer, devourer. Gather your power, for I will live forever. I will live for eter-nity. Gather your chains, and I will be free."

I tried to silence myself, to snuff out the spell that had ensnared me, but it was as futile as trying to hold back. The song curled around me like a vine, intertwining with my thoughts and emotions. I was utterly powerless to resist as the world around me began to shift. There was a hum of energy in the air, I could feel it pulsing through the soles of my shoes, a deep, resonant vibration that sent ripples through the earth.

It was a gathering of forces beyond my comprehension. The wind whipped around us, wild and wailing, like a chorus of tortured souls harmonizing with my melody, and the branches of the tree swayed, its limbs moving as if it were participating in this strange waltz.

As I continued to hum, my body moved without thought, swaying beneath the silver glow of the moonlight. My arms rose and fell gracefully, caught in a spell of both joy and darkness. For a moment, everything was exquisite—a bittersweet blend of liberation and dread. But that fleeting moment twisted into confusion.

What's happening? Is this how I go out? The thought riveted me. I was trapped in Lilly's body, lost to the darkness in the middle of nowhere. But my reverie shattered when a twig snapped to my left.

I froze, my eyes darting toward the tree line. As if summoned by my anxiety, Xander stepped out from the shadows, silhouetted against the pale moonlight. My breath hitched in my throat as horror washed over me.

His clothes were drenched in gore, splattered in crimson, and the remnants of violence shadowed his hands and face, painting him in a macabre hue. Blood dripped from his fingers like a grotesque offering, and my stomach twisted violently at the sight.

He had killed those people. There was no doubt about it. As soon as the thought entered my mind, a wicked grin spread across his face.

"There you are, my love. Bathing in the moonlight, are we?" He spoke gently, yet I sensed the malice in them.

Regardless, a smile split across my face. "I've been waiting for you, my darling." He crossed the clearing, closing the distance between us. And as he drew near, the dark look in his eyes had me wanting to bolt. There was no color, only darkness. Slowly, he reached out, cupping my face in his blood-soaked hands. "You're beautiful, as always."

My cheeks flushed at the compliment as his eyes roamed over my body, even as I recoiled inwardly. He moved closer, pressing his lips to my forehead. "Come, that house may have been destroyed, but I had a new one built for us over the years."

Over the years? He's been building a cabin out here for years? Why? He grasped my hand, leading me deeper into the trees. And we emerged to see my cabin. But not. It was new, fresh, and beautiful.

Xander had built the home my parents had left to me. How? Why? "It's beautiful," I whispered. A smile tugged at his lips. "I'm delighted you're pleased, my love. This will be our little hunting ground, where we'll choose your hosts once we've departed. It's a perfect plan—less suspicious for the townsfolk."

He wanted to keep killing people. To possess them. But why? The answer came to me with a sickening realization. "Because you love me. And you'll do anything to be with me. Even if it means hurting others."

Lilly

I stood in Emma's body, a strange cocktail of emotions swirling within me. Excitement ignited my veins—a thrilling rush of power at my fingertips, as if I could shape the world to my will. But, nestled within, was a pang of guilt, a sticky thread of regret weaving tightly around my heart.

This shouldn't be any different from the other victims I've possessed over the centuries. After all, plenty had come and gone before her, mere vessels that I'd borrowed and abandoned without a second thought. But something about Emma was special.

Her spirit had a spark, a resilience that had thwarted my attempts to get under her skin, to break her. No one else had reacted quite like she did, but now? She was completely broken. And trapped in the cage I meticulously crafted in her mind.

A prison forged from her fears and my dark desires. And yet, despite my plan to snuff out her soul as I took over, she was still fighting. It had been months of torment, biding my time like a predator waiting for Xander's arrival.

Yet here she was—showing me kindness even as I plotted her downfall. She had a light that pierced the gloom of centuries of darkness surrounding me, and it was as puzzling as it was maddening. But the truth hung like an anchor in my chest.

I had repaid her friendship by stealing her life. What have I become over these long centuries? Each thought sent a ripple of pain through me, a growing awareness that I might not be as heartless as I'd hoped to be. "Lillith, what are you doing?"

Xander's voice sliced through my thoughts, and his fingers brushed my cheek, wiping away a single tear I hadn't realized had slipped free. His touch was electric, and as I glanced into his eyes—no, Alex's eyes—seeing the man I loved so long ago. My first, and only love.

The man who had sworn that we would never lose our humanity. But we had, and it stung more than I wanted to admit. I shook my head, unable to answer him as the words became trapped in my throat. Instead, I wrapped my arms around his neck, pulling him close.

I buried my face in his chest, inhaling his scent—cinnamon and something darker, something haunting. He would be furious if he knew I had doubts, but the despair only dug deeper into my heart.

His arms wrapped around me, pushing away the emotions that had gathered beneath my skin. I could feel the steady thrum of his heart, and my breathing slowed, synchronizing with the rise and fall of his chest. For a moment, the world outside faded into the background.

"Lillith, what is wrong, my love?" he pressed again, his voice low and earnest. I shook my head again as tears brimmed in my eyes, trying desperately to keep my facade intact. Yet, it was as if a boulder had been pressed down on my shoulders.

The effort only made me feel more lost, adrift in a sea of turmoil. He stepped back, giving me space but holding my gaze with an intensity that dared me to reveal the truth. "Talk to me."

I hesitated, my thoughts slingshotting in every direction as I weighed my words like stones being tossed into water. Creating ripples of uncertainty. Finally, my voice emerged, a whisper barely breaking the surface. "I... I don't know if I can keep doing this." It was a silent confession, the words teetering on the brink of something monumental.

His expression darkened, the light in his eyes dimming as tension crackled between us. "What do you mean?" The question was clipped, and heavy like a thundercloud.

"Emma's still alive. She's fighting to stay alive."

Each word hung in the air like a weighty secret, the shame of my admission biting into my chest as I spoke it aloud. His body stiffened instantly, and the atmosphere shifted sharply around us. His eyes narrowed down to pinpricks of something I'd never seen in him before.

"She's still in there?"

I nodded slowly, my heart racing as I gauged his reaction. I could see the gears in his mind turning—a mixture of anger and disbelief crossing his features. "What do you mean she's fighting?" he challenged, his voice rising slightly. Each syllable dripped with a mixture of incredulity and mounting fury.

I stepped back, feeling the urge to retreat, yet I stood firm. "She's not dead. I can feel her resisting. It's like she's scratching at the walls of my mind, trying to break free." His expression morphed, a clash of emotions playing out across his features.

His fists clenched at his sides, the tension in his jaw tightening as realization dawned on him. "You let her live?" His words were like a knife twisting into my heart. "It wasn't on purpose, but I don't think I can do this. She's different. She was my friend." He gripped my shoulders, his fingers digging into my skin.

"You can. And you will." His words were an ice bath. And I knew he would never let me give Emma her body back. It was evident in his words, his grip. And It hurt to know he didn't care about my feelings. He continued, his voice laced with anger.

"I told you that we had to be ruthless. That we had to do whatever it took to survive. You said you understood. Are you telling me you lied? You betrayed me?" I shook my head slowly, shocked by his outburst. "No. I understand." I whispered, at a loss for words. "But I never wanted this. I never wanted to hurt people. And we have. A lot of

60

people." My words tumbled out as fear gripped my heart. His fists tightened so hard that the knuckles turned white, veins bulging like angry serpents along his forearms. He took a step toward me, and I shrunk back. "I don't understand. Why would you keep her alive? We need to stay together. We always do it this way." His eyes bore into mine.

"I know. But this is different. She was my friend, I guess in a way, I never wanted her dead to begin with. I'd just been too stupid to see it." Tears welled up in my eyes now. I was a fool to believe reasoning with him would have any effect.

He shook his head, disgust written all over his face. "Come on. We're getting out of here. Now." Before I could protest, he grabbed my arm and dragged me to Alex's truck. Although Alex was surely gone by now–Xander never had problems with his hosts living past the ritual, and usually neither had I. Why had Emma been able to? Was it because of me?

I let him pull me to the truck pushing me in. I wasn't focused on that though, My guilt and fear grew until I couldn't help trying to reach her. "Emma?" I call out inside my mind, hoping for a response.

The only sound that answered were my own screaming thoughts. I don't understand. I can feel her. But I don't know where she is. I glanced out the window as Xander pulled out of the clearing, heading to the road that led to the cabin.

How could I have been so stupid mentioning Emma? It would have been better to just ignore it, and keep going with our plan. We rode in silence, the tension in the air almost suffocating me.

I kept my eyes fixed on the road ahead, and after what seemed like an eternity. We finally pulled into the driveway of the cabin. Xander hopped out of the truck, slamming the door behind him, and I followed suit. Keeping my distance as we entered the house. Without warning, a wave of dread infiltrated my senses.

There was foreign energy floating through the air, along with an indescribable feeling of someone watching us. "Lil?" Xander called out. I turn to see him staring at me, the hardness replaced with a look of longing, "come here my love. It'll be okay." I hesitated, unsure if he would still be fuming despite his relaxed demeanor. He held out his hand, beckoning me closer.

With a deep breath, I took his hand, allowing him to pull me flush against his body. His lips brushed mine in a light, tender kiss, and I clung to the moment. This is the Xander I knew and loved. The sweet man that couldn't keep his hands off of me. The familiarity of his touch comforted me. Yet Emma's presence lingered, a constant reminder that she's still fighting for her life while I ignored her dying soul. And then there's Xander, despite his attitude now, he's changed somehow.

"Let me go," I whispered quietly. But his grip only tightened, the intensity in his eyes making me flinch. "I'll never let you go, Lil. You're mine, forever."

His words were like a steel cage had just locked around me, but that's not what made a shiver run down my spine. "No, Xander, someone's watching us. I can feel it."

His body stiffened beneath my arms as his gaze scanned the room. Expression hardening. He released me, stalking toward the front door. "I'm going to check the perimeter. Stay here."

I nodded as he clicked the door shut behind him. I could hear his footsteps making their way around the cabin, checking for any signs of trouble.

Suddenly, Emma's voice popped into my head out of nowhere. *Help me!* "Em?" I whispered, feeling a pang of hope.

But only silence followed. She sounded desperate, scared... completely alone. But the cage I made wasn't meant for communication. And I couldn't simply open or break through it. She was stuck. A moment later, Xander returned, his face flushed and his breaths were heavy.

"There's no one out there," he said, his voice strained. "But I found this." He pulled a piece of parchment from his pocket and handed it to me. The paper was old and yellowed, its edges frayed and tattered. "What is it?"

"A message, I assume," he said, his words clipped as he clenched his jaw. I watched him lift the parchment, reading aloud as the air got colder. Yet somehow, his voice remained low and steady. "The past cannot be forgiven. The blood cannot be cleansed. You defy what is natural, and for that, you must amend. Signed, the Coven of Flame and Shadows." I leaned in closer. "What do they mean? What did we do to make them so mad?" He shrugged, the parchment trembling slightly in his hands. "Does it matter? They're a bunch of old fools. They won't dare attack us."

He sounded confident, but I sensed the tension seeping from him—his hands balled into fists at his sides, betraying his bravado. I couldn't shake the feeling in the pit of my stomach, this was a warning. "Are you sure about that? What if they do?"

"Then we'll deal with it. Together, but I'm not going to let anyone take you from me." His words were meant to be reassuring, but it seemed more like a death sentence. And I wondered... if the Coven knew about the Soul Eater spell, about what we had been doing for the past couple of centuries, would they consider us monsters? Would they hunt us down? Or. Would they help me free Emma? I bit my lip, torn between my fear and my guilt, as an idea started to take root.

Emma

The days I spent living within Lilly's memories blurred together, creating a disorienting array of experiences that felt all too real. Sometimes, I wondered if this was my life now. Watching her dance and sing under the full moon, casting spells, and soaking up joy—it was both strange and enticing. I envied the way she embraced life, casting aside fear and doubt like an old pair of shoes. And the love she shared with Xander? It was nearly enough to make me believe in true love.

Almost. But then night would fall, and haunting screams would rip through the beautiful memories—visions of people being burned, tortured, and sacrificed that seeped into my mind like a dark poison. Those memories were relentless and horrifying.

I understood the weight of the sacrifices they made, the choices they had to live with. And it was no wonder why Lilly had lost herself along the way. They had done terrible things, but at every turn, they fought fiercely to protect each other, clinging to the idea of an eternity together. In a twisted sort of way, it was romantic.

But some of these memories told another tale, revealing Xander for what he truly was—a possessive and jealous man, obsessed with keeping Lilly by his side. He gave off a vibe that he would never let her go, not even if she wanted to leave. His dependency to her was dangerously consuming; threatening to crush them both.

As I sat up, stretching and rubbing the sleep from my eyes, a sliver of sunlight crept through the window, casting a golden glow across the room. Xander's arm draped over my waist as he stirred, pulling me closer, burying his face in the crook of my neck. His warm breath sent shivers racing down my spine.

Sometimes it was impossible to discern Lilly's senses from my own. The longer I was here, the more our emotions, and senses seemed to blend together. Carefully, I untangled myself from his embrace and slipped out of bed, reaching for my clothes and heading to the bathroom.

After quickly changing and brushing my teeth, I caught a glimpse of myself in the mirror, where Lilly's emerald eyes stared back at me. This was my life now. And a part of me hoped that someday, someone would find me, that I wouldn't be trapped in this body, reliving someone else's reality. Once I showered and got dressed, I crept down the hallway into the kitchen.

It was silent until Xander's voice came from the top of the stairs, making me jump. "Good morning, my love. You're up early." I turned, taking in his disheveled appearance, with a smile spreading across my face. "Good morning. Are you hungry? I can make breakfast if you'd like, or we could check out that new café that opened today?"

He chuckled, wrapping his arms around my waist and pulling me close. "Whatever you want, my dear." My heart fluttered at his sweet tone, and for a moment, I forgot myself. Savoring the warmth of Lilly's life. But then guilt rushed in, heavy and suffocating.

This wasn't my life, my body, or my love. It was just a memory—one I had no control over. "

"Let's go to the café." My tone was light, carefree. "I've heard they make amazing scones." I watched as he chuckled, kissing my forehead."

"That sounds perfect, my love." A rush of happiness filled my chest, almost blinding. And in a way, I was grateful. I had the chance to see Lilly for who she truly was, even if it meant losing myself in the process.

The Coven Of Flame And Shadow

Lilly

I stood, frozen, as I watched flames consume the cabin. Twisting and dancing against the pitch-black sky. The fire crackled, bright and alive, casting chaotic shadows around the forest. The suffocating scent of charred wood and burning memories clawed at my throat. But my legs were leaden, as if shackled to the ground.

Our home—the sanctuary we had nurtured for centuries—transformed into a raging inferno before our eyes. Echoes of laughter and warmth lingered in fading corners, burning away piece by piece. And panic gnawed at my insides.

Then a thought struck me. Emma possessed one thing she held near and dear, a picture of her and her parents. The only picture she had of them together. It appeared to me as clearly as the flames. Tacked to the corkboard above the kitchen table, their smiles bright and full of love. It was the only picture she had left of them.

I couldn't let it burn. I wouldn't. Without thinking, I darted toward the cabin. The heat wrapped around me like a scorching furnace as my feet pounded against the burning floorboards. I pushed through the doorway, flames licking at my skin. But I continued, squinting through the haze. The kitchen cabinets were engulfed in a fiery glow, pots and pans melted into grotesque shapes.

The corkboard was teetering on the edge of destruction, without a second thought, and I lunged for it. Reaching out as heat blazed around me. My fingers grazed the rough wood, stinging from the warmth, but I held on tight to the picture, yanking it free just as a burst of flames erupted nearby.

Fire rushed at me, and I stumbled back. A sharp pain shot up my arm when a piece of metal scraped my shoulder. The oven must have exploded, I thought, as the flames climbed higher. I held the picture close to my chest, and for a second, panic took over.

The entryway was obstructed by a section of the crumbled ceiling, and the other side of the house was engulfed in flames. I shut my eyes, focusing on steadying my breathing. It would be alright.

I could phase through the wall—I had done it before and could do it again. Just then, a beam collapsed in front of me, unleashing a wave of blistering air that hit my face. The fire was closing in fast.

My heart raced, thoughts spiraling in chaos. My only option was to escape through the window. Turning, I leapt through it, glass shattering and cutting into my skin. I squeezed my eyes shut as my body hit the ground. The impact knocking the wind out of me.

I lay there for a moment, coughing and gasping for air as the night sky swirled above, stars flickering like dying embers. "Hey! Are you alright?" Xander knelt beside me, his voice strained, a mix of relief and anger. "What the hell were you thinking? You almost got yourself killed!" I winced as I sat up, the heat from the fire still burning my skin.

"I had to, Em—" Before I could finish, he cut me off with a sharp glare that held all the frustration of our situation. "You risked your life? For a girl who should've been dead already? You'd let our memories fade away like that?" I opened my mouth to respond, but the words caught in my throat. Because the truth was, I didn't have an answer for what I did.

"What was I supposed to do? And what do we do now?" He shot me a determined look, his expression resolute. "We're getting out of here. But first? I'm going to make them pay!" His voice was fierce, burning with intensity like the flames swallowing our past. "Wait, what?" I took a step back, a mix of confusion and fear swirling in my gut. "If we run, we forfeit our lives. That was the condition of the soul eater spell. We can't leave town."

Xander looked at me, a glint of steel in his eyes. "Then we take the fight to them. We'll burn down their homes, take everything they hold dear. They'll regret messing with us." Chills skittered through my body. I was torn, caught between the chaos and the turmoil in my heart.

"Xander, come on. Killing more people isn't going to fix this. We can't keep doing this." He stepped closer, invading my space. His eyes blazed with fury as he gripped my shoulders with fingers capable of crushing bones.

For a brief moment, his desperation surged through me, a violent wave pulling me into its current. "Stop talking. You will do what I say. Do you understand?" His voice was low but commanding, a thunderstorm brewing in his eyes. "Stop, you're hurting me." The photograph slipped from my grip for a second, and in that moment, my emotions were let loose inside me.

A moment of vulnerability and weakness all in one. The heat surrounding us was no longer solely from the fire. It pulsed between our souls, resonating with everything that had come before. He let go, stepping back as if my words had stung him. Quickly, I scrambled to retrieve the picture, desperate to protect Emma's smiling face from the encroaching chaos.

"I can say the same about you. You've changed," he muttered, more to himself than to me. His words hit like a punch, while tears pricked at my eyes. "Look at everything that's happening. This isn't who I am. I can't follow you into madness—not again."

He shot me a challenging look. "You think you can act like you're the good witch now? Who are you?"

"Someone who won't kill an innocent girl," I shot back, my voice trembling despite my best efforts to remain strong. "I can't—no, I won't. Emma needs to be saved, and I think the coven is our best shot at that. I won't kill them, or her."

He struggled to understand what I was saying, caught off guard by the conviction behind them. "You really think she's that special? We've killed plenty without a second thought." Frustration swept over me like a tide, fueled by the raw emotion crackling between us.

"You don't understand! I've lost enough, and I can't do this anymore. Emma's life hangs in the balance because of our choices." I took a step back, my heart pounding in my chest. "This—this isn't love. It's a twisted obsession, and I won't follow you down this path anymore."

As I straightened my spine, magic thrummed beneath the surface of my skin. For a fleeting moment, Xander seemed to notice it; his eyes widening in realization. "Don't you dare abandon me!"

His words echoed inside me, but I knew I had to be firm. "I can't be what you want. I won't throw away my soul any more than I already have to stand beside you. Goodbye, Xander." I whispered it, feeling my heart shatter as I did.

Closing my eyes, I chanted the teleportation spell, hoping it would pull me away from the chaos. "In a swirl of light, I rise. Whispers of the past in the skies. Open doors to where I deem." The air shimmered, and in an instant, I was pulled into the spell—whisked away from the fiery wreckage of the cabin and everything it had stood for.

When I finally landed in the woods, the cold bit into my skin, snapping me back to reality. I crumpled to the ground, tears streaming down my cheeks as I gasped for breath. My heart felt like it had exploded, and the pain was like nothing I had ever known. But now, I was alone.

I had to figure things out. Emma was still out there, alive, but at risk. I couldn't let that chance slip away. I was going to find the coven, plead for her life, and if they turned me down, I'd show them what I was capable of.

Focused on that thought, I took a deep breath. But first, I needed to track them down.

Emma

My hand reached up to tuck a loose strand of golden hair behind my ear. Today seemed different, electric. And I couldn't quite put my finger on why. I was ten years old, seeing the world through the bright, innocent lens of childhood.

The scent of baking bread and herbs wafted through Lilly's grandmother's kitchen, wrapping around me like a warm hug, and I could hardly contain my excitement. "Are you ready, Lillith?" The gentle voice jolted me from my thoughts.

I looked up to see an older woman smiling down at me, her warm eyes glowing with affection. I saw the resemblance already—same bright emerald eyes, matching wide smile. "Yes, Grandma, I'm ready." The excitement bubbled in my chest as she rummaged around in a drawer, her movements light and spirited.

Finally, she pulled out a long, thin box and held it out to me as if it were something precious. Taking the box felt like holding a secret, and I hesitated for a second. My mind conjuring up thoughts of what it could be. And then I opened it. A gasp escaped my lips at what lay inside: a stunning wand made of shiny evergreen wood.

At the tip sat a large bloodstone, pulsing softly as if it had a heartbeat of its own. "Is this for me?" I asked, barely able to contain my disbelief. "It is," she beamed. "I've been saving it for you. It belonged to your great-great-grandmother."

The magic of the moment enveloped me, and something stirred deep inside me. "Is today really the day I learn how to use it?" The words were heavy and exciting on my tongue. "Absolutely. Today is your day to shine, my dear." Her eyes sparkled with a mix of mischief and pride.

"But remember, every witch has her own style for casting spells. Some chant, some hum, and some even sing." She winked at me. "Let's see what yours is. Shall we?"

"I've never used magic before..." A wave of self-doubt washed over me. "You have—just not with this." She offered the wand, and as I took it, warmth surged through my fingers, going down to my toes. It felt as if it recognized me, like we had been waiting for this moment. "Now, this wand will bond with you. Its magic will only listen to you and you alone."

"Won't I get in trouble?"

"No way," she laughed, shaking her head. "This is a family heirloom. And I'm passing it down to you, like a gift that keeps on giving. One day, you'll give it to your daughter, and she'll do the same."

Her smile turned soft, nostalgic. "And do you remember that star birthmark on your wrist? It's a sign of hope and great things for your future." My heart soared as I nodded, gripping the wand tightly. "Okay. What should I do?"

"Let's start with a simple levitation spell," she suggested, pointing to a shimmering glass orb resting on the table, reflecting bits of light like a tiny star. I took a deep breath, adjusting my grip on the wand as energy hummed in the air. "What's next?" I asked, glancing up at her.

"Close your eyes and focus. Picture the orb floating in the air," she instructed, her voice soothing as she moved to lean back against the counter. With my eyes closed, I could almost see the orb lifting. "And remember, every spell needs a little rhythm," she added.

"Just like a song. Try this one. Light as air, rise from there, lift this item without a snare. Move through space, gentle as lace, By my will,

71

so mote it be." I took a deep breath and hummed the tune, a catchy, whimsical melody that felt as if it belonged to the wind itself. As I sang the words, the wand warmed in my grip, buzzing delightfully in my veins.

It was as if the air vibrated with magic. To my amazement, the orb quivered slightly, and a smile spread across my face as the enchantment filled the room.

It was magical. But as I began to lose myself within the moment, Grandma called out from the kitchen. "Lillith, dear. That's enough for now. I need to go check on dinner." She turned her back to me, gathering a few things from the fridge. Her soft smile made it hard to complain, and as much as I wanted to continue, I knew better. "Why don't you go play for a bit? I'll call you when it's ready," she added over her shoulder.

I nodded, reluctantly placing the orb back on the table. The excitement from the spell slowly faded away, replaced by the importance of my next adventure. Gathering my colorful plastic figurines and plush animals, I climbed the creaking staircase to my room. Sunlight streamed through the window, casting a warm, inviting glow across the space.

I set my toys on the plush rug and submerged myself in a world of make-believe. Yet, even as I lost myself in play, something stirred in my heart—a blend of nostalgia and a longing for a time when I could be free. I clung tightly to Lilly's carefree moment, letting it guide me away from my worries.

Suddenly, my imaginative world was interrupted by an unfamiliar noise filtering through the open window. Curiosity nudged at me, pulling me away from my toys. I abandoned my playtime and wandered over to the window, peering outside.

What I saw made my heart race. In the distance, a figure dressed entirely in black moved stealthily into the woods, their form cutting a striking silhouette against the vibrant greens and browns of the landscape. Who could it be?

The intrigue gnawed at my insides, drawing me toward the door like a moth to a flickering flame. Quietly, I crept down the stairs, conscious of every creak and groan beneath my feet. As I stepped onto the porch, a cool breeze wrapped around me, sending a shiver down my spine.

I could hear the distant chirping of cicadas and the whisper of leaves rustling in the gentle wind. Carefully, I closed the door behind me, taking a tentative step off the porch. I was mindful not to trip over gnarled roots or stumble on the occasional fallen branch that littered the ground. The deeper I went, the more I lost track of time, caught in the web of the woods' embrace. A sudden sound flitted to my left, pulling me back to reality.

I spotted the figure in black walking deeper into the shadows, slipping between the towering trees and fading from sight. Instinct took over. I quickened my pace, slipping behind a cluster of bushes as the thrill of discovery surged through me.

I had to know who he was. Just as I was beginning to feel like I was chasing a dream, the figure turned around. I froze, panic flooding through me. "I know you're there," he called out, his voice rich and clear. Emerging from the shadows was a boy, about my age. His long black hair flowed like waves caught in the breeze.

His eyes were a mesmerizing shade of deep green, sparkling with mischief and curiosity. It was as if I had stumbled upon something I wasn't meant to see. "Hi," I managed, lifting my hand in an awkward wave.

He raised an eyebrow, a fleeting grin tugging at the corners of his mouth as he walked closer, inspecting me. "What are you doing out here? Are you following me?" His tone was teasing, yet there was a sincerity beneath it. I hesitated, my cheeks flushing. "Yes? No! I saw you and got curious."

The confession spilled out of my mouth before I could stop it. He chuckled, the sound warm and inviting, and extended his hand towards me. "I'm Alexander, but you can call me Xander. It's a lot simpler."

"Lillith, but everyone calls me Lilly." I blurted out, feeling shy yet emboldened by his easy smile. He grinned wider, even nodding slightly as if my name held importance. "I think I like Lillith better. It's a beautiful name for a beautiful girl." His words caressed me like sunlight on a chilly morning, igniting warmth within.

"Do you want to be my friend?" A bubble of excitement blossomed in my chest at the prospect. "Sure," I replied, as that familiar fidgeting energy that came from wanting more.

With that simple question, laughter exploded around us, our voices weaving in and out as we played among the trees. We spun tales of daring escapades and bravery, the sun beginning its descent and painting the sky in breathtaking hues of orange and purple.

But soon the spell of time snapped, and I knew I had to return home. "Will I see you tomorrow?" Xander asked, his voice threaded with hope. I smiled brightly at him as his eyes sparkled in the moonlight.

"Yes." With that promise lingering in the air, I turned toward home. I could feel Lilly's essence, light and carefree. The rush of a new budding friendship made her lighter than ever. It was nice to see her like this, normal and happy.

Of Magic And Souls

Lilly

I had a small cabin built at the edge of town, a cozy little refuge tucked away from prying eyes. It was my safety net, a place I could slip into when the world threatened to overwhelm me. But today, I was grateful for it more than ever. With a heavy heart, I pushed the door open, letting out a sigh of relief as the familiar scent of my drying herbs filled the air, soothing my frayed nerves.

It wasn't much to look at—a few battered shelves along the left wall lined with crystals, potion ingredients, and the odd volume on magical theory. On the right, a fireplace, and a small couch resting in front of it, welcoming me like an old friend. In the corner stood a round table strewn with half-finished projects, and at the back, a miniature kitchen where I often brewed teas and concoctions.

But it was home now, my little sanctuary from the storm brewing outside. As I sank into the couch, I couldn't shake the image of Xander from my mind. The hurt I had seen in his eyes was like daggers twisting in my chest. I remembered how he'd grabbed me, and for a moment, fear had crept in, a whisper suggesting that he might hurt me.

And in other ways, perhaps he already had. A deep, gaping emptiness settled within me, echoing with the silence of centuries spent intertwined, each moment woven into my being. Now, those threads lay frayed and brittle, leaving me to confront the vast void of my heart. I slumped deeper into the couch, not knowing what to do, or where to go. The only certainty I had was that I couldn't let Emma die. And that the coven might hold the answers I sought. They were my best chance of reversing what I'd done.

I scanned the cabin, trying to conjure a plan. "I could track them, but what if I'm walking into a death trap? How do I even find them?" I pondered. Scrying was an option, but it came with risks. Still, it was my only shot. With that thought in mind, I rose from the couch and made my way to the shelves, searching through jars and vials for what I needed.

I gathered a map of the forest, a crystal for focus, and herbs—marjoram, sage, and lavender—each chosen for their protective and clarifying qualities. Once I laid everything out on the table, I took a moment to steady myself, forcing myself to breathe deeply.

Closing my eyes, I focused on the crystal in my hand. Its coolness contrasted with the heat rising inside me. "Guide my eyes, clear my mind, bring forth what I seek. By the stars and the sea, let thy spirits come to me. Guide me to the coven's home. Open my eyes to the unknown."

As I recited the words, the air shifted, pulsating with energy that seemed to swirl like a dark storm. It spun in chaotic patterns, making me feel dizzy, and I gripped the table for support, trying to keep my balance.

Then, within the haze, a vision began to spin into focus—a winding path cutting through the shadowy woods, leading to a fairy circle bathed in a strange glow. My heart raced as I took in the details.

In the center stood a cloaked figure, their whispers weaving through the trees, incantations layered with a power that made the very night seem to tremble around them. But as quickly as it materialized, the figure vanished, slipping through my fingers like sand.

I gasped, swallowing air as my knees buckled beneath me. Stumbling back to the couch, I clutched my head as disorientation washed over me. It was overwhelming, but I reminded myself that I was close—so very close. All I had to do now was follow that path, and with a bit of luck, I might actually uncover their secrets.

Failure wasn't an option. The consequences of that were too bleak to even consider. Glancing at the time, I was surprised to see that it was early morning—the world still enveloped in twilight. Quickly, I gathered my supplies, black cohosh for clarity, nettle to fortify me against harm, and my black tourmaline crystal, a shield against negativity.

Wrapping it all in a cloth satchel, I slung it around my neck and whispered, "Protect my body and mind, so it shall be." I hoped it would be enough to guard me against whatever awaited me. With that, I stepped out of the safety of my cabin and into the night. The wind howled through the trees, and a haunting tune that hinted at an approaching storm, sending a shiver down my spine.

As I made my way into the woods, the familiar crunch of leaves underfoot was swallowed by the sounds of the forest coming alive. Shadows danced on the narrow path, and the gnarled roots seemed to reach out to me. The deeper I ventured, the more the light from the moon flickered in and out of view through the dense foliage overhead. It was getting harder to see, so I raised my hand and whispered a small spell, summoning a soft glow that lit up the area.

After what seemed like hours of winding through the twisting path, I emerged into a clearing that had been plucked from a dream. A perfect ring of white and pink mushrooms. Their caps curving upwards like tiny, beaming umbrellas. They formed a circle that shimmered under the glow of my spell. The edges sparkled like dewdrops, catching the light and shining like tiny pearls. As I stood there, I couldn't help but notice a soft hum in the air, brushing against the back of my mind. Drawn in by the magic in the air, I took a step closer, not wanting to look away. Standing right on the edge, I felt my breath catch in my throat.

There was this irresistible pull, almost like the circle was calling my name, tempting me to jump in. After a quick moment of doubt, I decided to go with my instincts. I took a deep breath, stepping over the line of mushrooms, and in an instant, everything shifted. The air felt strange, charged with something thrilling and a bit unsettling at the same time, like the flutter of a thousand butterflies taking flight. But before I could fully absorb what was happening, a bright light engulfed me, swallowing me whole. It happened so fast. I was weightless, floating in a void of pure energy.

The sensation overwhelmed me, filling every inch of my body. Then, as suddenly as it had begun, the feeling was gone. I found myself sprawled out on a cold stone floor, contrasting the softness of the moss I had been standing on. Everything was dark, the air thick with the smell of burning wax mixed with something funky that reminded me of burnt toast.

I blinked, trying to focus through the haze, and then I saw them—three cloaked figures looming over me, their shadows twisting and writhing like smoke. Rubbing my eyes, I took in their sharp cheekbones and piercing gazes, the energy radiating from them unmistakably screaming, "Stay away." But this was the price of the choices I had made, and I was in too deep to turn back now.

Each of them had intricate tattoos on their left wrists that instantly caught my eye. The first guy, who was a massive figure, stepped forward. "Lillith, what an unexpected surprise." I couldn't help but notice his tattoo—a scale balancing a skull and a heart, along with a couple of big 'XX's.' He continued, "I'm Bram, the Keeper of Balance. So, what's brought you to our little hideout?"

His eyes skewered into me, making my insides twist with anxiety. I knew I had to tread carefully. They had no reason to trust me, and I wasn't even sure they'd be willing to help. But hey, they hadn't killed me yet, so maybe there was still hope.

"I need your help," My voice wavered slightly, despite my attempt to sound confident. "I'm sure you already know I've taken over Emma Cross's body. But she's still alive somewhere in here, and I need the coven's help to save her."

The silence that followed was like a heavy weight, each of them regarding me with varying degrees of skepticism. After nearly an eternity, Bram spoke again, his tone dripping with barely concealed disdain. "And why should we help you? You're nothing but a parasite." The words stung, but I knew better than to let my emotions get the best of me. Keeping a level head was critical. "Because Emma is innocent in all of this. You'd be helping her, not me. I'd go back to being a specter, a ghost."

I could see the gears in their minds turning over my words. Finally, the man leaning against the wall, his tattoo a crown with jewels and the number IV inscribed above it, spoke up.

"I say we help her, Bram. If she's telling the truth and Emma is alive, then I don't want her death to be in our hands." Bram narrowed his eyes at the man but seemed to be considering his words. After a few more moments of agonizing silence, he sighed, looking over at the other man whose tattoo was a lion's head, its number VIII, hovering above it. "Kael, what do you think?"

"I get Alistair's point," he said, his voice deep and gravelly, giving off some serious authority vibes. "I think it's definitely worth discussing with the others. They deserve to know what's happening." As he spoke, I noticed the looks exchanged between them—they all seemed to be on the same page. It felt like a silent agreement brewing.

Bram turned to me, his face set in a stoic expression, eyes piercing, as if searching for any hint of deceit. He leaned in slightly. "We will discuss this with the others," his tone held steady. "But until then, you're staying with the coven." He held my gaze, his voice dropping to a lower, more dangerous tone. "If you try to run... we'll hunt you down and deal with you without a second thought. Understood?"

I nodded, not knowing what else to say. I didn't know what the future held for me, but I was determined to do whatever it took to save Emma. As Bram at last turned to leave, Kael moved to my side, his demeanor a strange mixture of formal, yet calm.

"Protocol, no hard feelings," he drawled, his words barely registering before he reached out, touching my forehead. Suddenly, a flash of light exploded behind my eyes. And everything went black.

Emma

Here, time had no concept. Forward was back, back was sideways. All I knew was that Xander and Lilly had hung out every day since they met. Their bond deepened with each passing moment. The sun was setting, spilling oranges and pinks across the sky as if someone had punctured the heavens with a paintbrush.

I found myself in Grandma's garden, the air thick with the aromatic smells of her precious herbs—chamomile, lavender, you name it. "Lilly!" Grandma's voice brought us back to reality, her arms crossed, and her emerald eyes were sharp like daggers.

"What are you doing out here? You need to focus on your studies. A witch's knowledge is only built on dedication and discipline." I could feel Lilly's rebellious spirit rising, and I shot back, "Seriously? You want me to sit here and chant the same old spells? Do you really think that's all there is to magic?"

Her face tightened, and I could sense the tension rising within them both. "Magic is not a game. You know the rules—" I rolled my eyes. "Yeah, yeah, rules. Xander says I can do more, be something more. He believes in me."

"Xander?" Her tone shifted, tinged with disapproval. "That boy is a bad influence. He's leading you down a dark path. You mustn't let him distract you from your training."

"Distract me?" I laughed. "You mean open my eyes to what magic can really do? He's shown me things—new spells, unbridled power. And honestly? I think you're scared of what I can do.

Her brows furrowed slightly, and her lips pressed together in a thin line as she spoke. "I am trying to protect you, Lillith." She took a half-step closer, her shoulders tense. "I've spent years learning the right way to wield magic." As she continued, her gaze dropped momentarily, softening her expression. "You can't dive into the unknown without understanding the consequences." She straightened her posture, but the tremor in her voice hinted at the hurt lingering beneath the surface.

"Maybe you've got it wrong then. What if there's more to magic than simply following some boring rules? Xander makes me feel alive. And when I'm with him, I don't feel trapped."

As Grandma stepped closer, her brow furrowed in a mixture of anger and grief. "You're young. You don't yet understand how delicate the balance of these things can be. With dark magi—"

"Dark magic? Why do you treat it like it's some monster lurking under the bed?" I fired back. "Maybe embracing it could help me become someone greater. Someone who others would remember." The moment I uttered those words, Lilly's heart raced—she really believed in what Xander had been feeding her.

"Just because it feels exciting now, doesn't mean it's the right thing to do," she whispered, stepping back as if my words struck her. "Once you cross that line, there's no coming back. And you'll regret it."

"Regret what?" I scoffed. "Living a half-life? Following outdated traditions?" With a softer tone, I placed my hand on her arms. "Grandma, I want to explore who I am—not who you want me to be. You can't keep me in a bubble forever.."

The silence stretched between us like a chasm, And I could see the lines of worry deepening in her grandmother's face, her brows knitting together as her lips trembled ever so slightly. Her eyes, usually so bright, seemed dull. The corners of her mouth turned downward, and she pressed a trembling hand to her chest, as if trying to steady the ache within. There was a battle raging inside me as well, and I could feel

Lilly's regret, her hesitance, yet an all-consuming stubbornness pushed her forward.

"Lilly..." Grandmother's voice cracked. "I can't allow you to do this. I won't watch you throw your life away for some dark warlock. He doesn't care about you, or your future."

My jaw clenched tightly, and I felt heat rushing to my cheeks as my hands balled into fists at my sides. "You don't get to decide that!" I shot back, my voice rising sharply, each word laced with defiance. A bitter laugh escaped my lips, the sound harsh and almost incredulous. I stared her down, a pulse of frustration drumming in my temples. "I'm not a child anymore!" I spat, eyes blazing.

Grandma's shoulders slumped as she spoke, her gaze dropping for a moment before locking onto mine again. The corners of her mouth turned down, and I could see the sadness etched in her face. "If that's how you feel," she said softly, trying to keep her voice steady, "then go be with him."

The tension hung between us, and I could see the fear in her gaze. "But just remember," she continued, her voice barely above a whisper, "once you walk down that path, you might lose everything—including me." Her eyes held mine, pleading for me to understand.

For a fleeting moment, I could feel how heavy Lilly's heart was, but she was determined not to be swayed. "Maybe that's a risk I'm willing to take." With that, I turned, taking a step away from her toward the shadows.

Through the forest, I caught sight of Xander beyond the garden, leaning against a tree with that wild, carefree smile Lilly had come to crave. "You coming?" he called out, a spark dancing in his eyes that made her heart flutter. And just like that, she turned her back on the past, stepping into the dark with open arms.

Lilly

As soon as the light faded, I found myself in a room that felt like a strange mix of comfort and magic. The walls were painted in a soothing lavender, and the soft glow of the sun filtered through the window. The bed was draped in crisp, black, silky sheets. A white dresser stood against one wall holding an assortment of trinkets and tiny figurines, but it was the view outside the window that truly captured my attention.

Beyond the glass, a breathtaking garden stretched out, a paradise. Vivid flowers burst with dazzling colors. And at the heart stood a statue of a wizard. With a long, flowing beard that cascaded down his chest, and a robe adorned with shimmering silver stars. He looked like he had stepped out of a fairy tale. In one hand, he held a wand aloft, directing streams of water that sparkled like liquid diamonds.

Wooden beams arched over the pathways of the garden, each one draped with willow vines that flowed down, creating little alcoves where you could find a few benches. I could imagine curling up there with a good book or simply relaxing there for hours. "I hope this is okay. It'll be your room if we agree to help you." Kael's deep voice snapped me out of my daze. I turned to see him leaning in the doorway, arms casually crossed.

"It's beautiful," I replied, a smile spreading across my face as I spun slowly to take it all in.

Kael's posture relaxed a bit, the corners of his mouth lifting in a subtle grin, as if pleased to see my reaction. Then suddenly, the door swung open, and in walked a girl balancing a towering stack of clothes in her arms.

She moved with a graceful ease, her long, curly blonde hair cascading around her shoulders like a halo. As she lifted her gaze, her soft green eyes met mine, sparkling with a warmth that instantly made me feel welcomed. I noticed a tattoo on her left wrist—a delicate design of an angel pouring water that flowed gently down to her palm, with the number XIV inscribed above it.

It caught my eye, and I glanced back up just in time to see her smile, a hint of curiosity in her own expression. She shifted the stack slightly, her posture open and inviting as she stepped farther into the room.

Kael smiled at her and then looked back to me, probably sensing my confusion. "This is Ellie. She represents the tarot card, Temperance. She's the calmest, and most patient of the group," he explained with a hint of admiration in his voice.

"And this," he pointed to her wrist, "is her Catalyst, what defines her." Ellie gave me a shy smile as she set the clothes on the bed. "It's nice to meet you, Lillith," she said, performing a little curtsey.

I awkwardly bowed back, feeling unsure of the proper etiquette for a situation like this. She chuckled and waved her hand dismissively. "You don't have to do that. I'm not royalty or anything,"

"Oh, yeah. Sorry," I mumbled, suddenly aware of the heat creeping into my cheeks. I glanced down, nervously fiddling with the hem of my shirt. "It's okay," she replied, her smile brightening as she shifted the stack of clothes to one side, making room for herself in the doorway.

"If you need anything, my room is right across the hall." She took a small step forward, her eyes sparkling with friendliness. "You should come find me later." I nodded, a bit more at ease, and offered a shy smile in return. "Sure. Thanks." I watched her as she turned to leave, her hair trailing like ribbons behind her.

Kael shifted his weight, motioning to the pile of clothes on the bed. "I figured you might want to get out of those nasty rags," he grimaced, eyeing my torn and dirty outfit, which probably still smelled of charred wood. I glanced down at my burnt, torn clothes, and a fleeting sense of humiliation coursed through me. "Yes, thank you.

"No problem." He crossed his arms again, leaning against the wall with an effortless ease that suggested he was used to commanding attention. "I know this is a lot to take in, but I really do think you're here for a reason."

"Really? You don't think this is some elaborate scheme?" I asked as I shifted from foot to foot, crossing my arms defensively. He straightened up, channeling a more serious demeanor. "No, I'm quite confident it's not." His gaze intensified, as if weighing my every reaction. "Besides, I'm pretty good at reading people

A smirk began to tug at the corners of his mouth, and he raised an eyebrow playfully. "And I can tell there's more here than meets the eye."

"Okay, so, what happens now?" I run a hand through his hair, glancing toward the door as if contemplating the next steps physically. "Well, now, if we choose to help you. We would need to take you to the healer. And find out what condition Emma's soul is in, then go from there."

"That sounds like a good plan." Everything was moving so fast, but it felt nice to see they had a strategy in place—even if they hadn't fully agreed to help me yet. "Okay, well, what do I do until then?" I asked, glancing around the room as if the answer might materialize from the lavender walls.

He nodded thoughtfully, as though he were considering my question.

Then he pointed to the bathroom. "You can get washed up. And when you're done, relax and get used to your new abode." I arched my brow. "New abode? That sounds so official."

"I'm a man of many talents, one of which is being a master of vocabulary," he smirked, a playful glint in his eyes that made me shake my head, chuckling. "Okay. Thanks," I said, appreciating his lightheartedness. With one last smirk, he walked out, closing the door behind him.

I sighed, scanning the room once more. This was a lot to take in, but at least I wasn't being locked away. Hopefully the worst of it was over.

Catalyst Of Chaos

I stripped out of my filthy clothes, tossing them aside with a firm resolve to dispose of them as soon as possible. At the moment, I just wanted to get clean. Turning on the water in the shower, I let the stream warm up while I surveyed the bathroom.

The tiles matched the room's calming lavender tone, and the plush towels were a rich, deep purple. The air was fragrant with the scent of lilacs, and the counter was lined with an array of shampoos and soaps that promised a luxurious experience.

With a sigh escaping my lips, I stepped into the stream of water, letting it wash away the dirt, blood, and tension clinging to me like a second skin. The sensation was pure bliss, and my muscles finally relaxed. After a good scrubbing and washing my hair several times, I finally stepped out, wrapping a towel around myself, heading for the sink, and wiping the mirror down.

Emma's eyes stared back at me, a brilliant deep blue that reminded me of the ocean's darker depths. Her dark hair was still tangled and damp, hanging down her back like a curtain of waves. But as I looked into her eyes, a wave of anxiety rushed over me.

How could I possibly convince them to help me? Seriously, how does one persuade a group of strangers to take such a huge risk? And even if they did agree, what would happen if they couldn't bring Emma back? Would they blame me?

Deep down, I knew it was my fault for the mess I was in, but I had to remind myself that at least I was trying to make it right. After drying off, I pulled the clothes Ellie had brought me from the pile. The outfit was simple—a pair of black jeans and a dark green T-shirt. They were comfortable, and I appreciated the effort they'd put into making me feel welcome.

After a brief struggle with my hair, I decided to braid it to the side—practical and easy, a small victory in terms of looking somewhat presentable. I left the bathroom and flopped down on the edge of the bed, the softness of the sheets contrasting with the heaviness in my heart as I stared at the ceiling, I allowed myself to get lost in thought as I processed everything that had happened. Never in a million years did I think I'd find myself here, in a coven I didn't even know existed. But now that I was in the thick of it, I had to hope they'd truly help me. Time slipped away as I lay there, lost in contemplation, until the door creaked open once more.

I shot up, seeing a stunning woman standing in the doorway. Her presence was commanding, yet welcoming. She had a crescent moon tattoo surrounded by wild dandelions on her wrist, with a 'II' inked above it. Her long, flowing brown hair cascaded down her back, and her hazel eyes sparkled with a hint of mischief.

She was wearing a simple white dress that draped elegantly over her form, complemented by a black shawl. I jumped to my feet, suddenly battling an urge to bow or curtsy, but I only ended up stumbling, almost tripping, over my own feet.

She laughed, closing the door behind her. "Hello, I'm River. I represent The High Priestess. I know this room isn't much, but we weren't exactly expecting you."

"It's lovely, really," I said honestly. "That's good." Her expression turned serious, like she was preparing to reveal something monumental. "I assume you have questions." I nodded, eager to unleash the flood of inquiries swirling in my mind. "Yes, lots, actually."

"Well then," she said, crossing her arms. "First of all, we have agreed to help you. But you must be completely honest with us. No matter what."

"I will, I swear," I promised. "I've made a lot of mistakes in my life, but this one was by far the biggest." She nodded, her eyes softening with understanding.

"Very well. Secondly, the healer will need some time to evaluate the state of your friend's soul. I'll take you to her, and then we can see what we can do." With a flick of her wrist, a set of double doors that had been closed swung open. I squinted, peering inside to find a spacious walk-in closet lined with empty hangers and shelves.

"There's plenty of space for your belongings, and I can take you shopping for some new clothes once we get things figured out," she added. I stared at her in disbelief. "You're really going to do this for me?"

"It's the right thing to do," she replied. "You wouldn't be here if you weren't meant to be. And you won't even have to leave Mystic Hollows."

"Mystic Hollows?" I repeated, the name tickling my curiosity. "Yes. That's where we are. A realm unto its own. The only way in or out is through the fairy circle you arrived through from Weathersfield."

"How did I manage to get in, then?"

"Well, we had been hunting you down for a while, so we left it open for you to 'slip through,' so to speak," River explained. "And that actually works?" She laughed again, as if my question was the most adorable thing she'd heard all day. "Well, yes. We are witches, after all. It's not just about the circle itself but our collective magic allowing you to pass."

I shook my head, trying to wrap my mind around the concept. "Wow." River nodded.

"Yes. Well, let's cut the chit chat and get to business." She smiled and beckoned me to follow her. As we stepped into the hall, I was immediately struck by the sheer scale and beauty of the coven's space.

The hallway stretched out ahead, the ceiling soaring above us, and the walls were painted a calming white that made it feel serene. The floor, crafted from beautiful red cedar, added a warm glow to the ambiance, and the scent of cinnamon filled the air.

But what truly caught my attention were the paintings lining the corridor. Each depicted a different witch, bold strokes illustrating their unique tattoos and numbers. It was like I had stumbled into an art gallery dedicated to magic. "What are these?"

"The pictures honor our ancestors," River explained as we continued our walk. "Each one represents one of our past leaders. The major arcana are the original members, while the minor arcana are those we choose to join us." I stopped in front of one painting, my breath catching in my throat. The familiar face was hauntingly beautiful, eyes sparkling with a vibrant emerald just like mine.

"Mom?" I whispered, staring at the portrait of a woman whose long, golden hair cascaded down her shoulders, adorned with a flower crown, her hand placed delicately on her pregnant stomach.

River nodded, with a light smile tinged with sadness. "Yes. Your mother was a great witch. She was The Star, and she represented the number 17. The Star is a symbol of hope."

As I looked down at my wrist, at my birthmark, a flood of emotions washed over me. I couldn't help but wonder if Grandma had known all along. River followed my gaze, understanding shining in her eyes. "The star is your birthmark. But it hasn't been activated as the card. When you went down the path to darkness, you changed your fate."

I furrowed my brow, trying to process everything. "Why didn't my grandmother tell me about any of this?"

"She did try to," River replied. "But you were young, and she didn't want you to feel pressured into this. It's a lot to take on. I'm assuming that when the time came to tell you, you had already chosen your path."

"Yeah," I whispered, feeling a heavy guilt sinking deep within me like a stone tossed into a lake. "Don't dwell on it too much," River replied, her voice gentle but firm. "With time, it could activate. That all depends on you." She waved her hand dismissively.

"Anyway, shall we continue?" I nodded slowly, tearing my gaze away from my mom's picture, my mind swirling with questions. I wondered if she'd ever walked this very hall, carrying her own burdens, her own hopes.

As we continued down the corridor, I started to notice that the door frames were adorned with unique symbols and numbers. "What are these?" I asked, genuinely curious. River smiled, clearly excited to explain. "Oh, these are our rooms. Each one is designed specifically for the person it belongs to. For Kael, he is the Strength card. He's one of the leaders of the minor arcana, so he has a large room that connects with the library as well as an office. He uses that space a lot."

Her voice softened as she continued, "Ellie has a smaller room since she is Temperance; her element is water, and she likes calm, peaceful spaces." As she spoke, the surrounding atmosphere shifted, alive with the sounds of cheerful chatter and laughter echoing from the dining hall we were passing.

On the opposite side, a study room was scattered with scrolls and potions, the scent of herbal magic lingering in the air, and a grand library overflowing with more books than I could count. "There's a lot to explore here," River said as we stopped in front of a door with a symbol of a staff above, a snake coiling around it. River knocked gently, and the door creaked open.

Revealing a room bathed in dim light from glowing orbs that danced playfully throughout the space. "Mia, are you busy?" River called into the room. "Not at all," came a gentle voice. A woman turned to face us, her dark, curly hair pulled back into a loose bun.

She wore a flowing yellow shirt. With white pants. On her wrist, a tattoo of a dove diving into a cup, with a plus sign inscribed above it, caught my eye. "Lillith, this is Mia. She is the Ace of Cups."

"The bringer of blessings, and the start of beginnings. She is a powerful healer."

Mia extended her hand, and I took it, feeling an immediate warmth radiate from her. "It's a pleasure. I've heard about your precarious situation. Let's see what we can do, hm?"

I nodded and followed her to a long table set up with various candles and a vase of vibrant flowers. "You'll need to be in a meditative state for me to see what condition your friend is in," Mia explained.

"Oh, okay," I replied, trying to prepare myself for whatever was to come. "Please, lay back and get comfortable," she instructed, gesturing toward the table. I complied, reclining and looking up at the ceiling, unsure of what to expect.

Mia lit a candle, and the enchanting scent of lavender and vanilla wafted around the room, calming my racing thoughts. "Now, take a deep breath in and exhale," she said softly. I closed my eyes, focusing on the rhythm of my breathing, and tried to let the world outside fade away. "Clear your mind. Don't think about anything besides the sound of my voice. Now, let the world slip away. Allow yourself to drift," Mia instructed gently, her voice creating a tranquil space around us.

As the room faded into silence, I felt a sensation as if I were floating. "Good. Now you're going to feel my magic flow over you," she continued, her tone soothing yet powerful. "It won't hurt, but it might feel a little odd."

"Okay," I replied hesitantly, bracing myself for whatever was to come. Within minutes, I could feel a light sensation wash over me, reminiscent of being submerged in water. The coolness spread up my legs, arms, and chest, surrounding me until I felt like I was floating on my back in an endless ocean.

Then Mia inhaled sharply. Her voice dropped low. "She's trapped, deep within your mind, your memories. "She's in danger. If she reaches the end of your memories before we can pull her out, she will be gone forever.

My eyes flew open, heart racing as the weight of those words sank in. "Wait, how much time do we have?" I shot up from the table, shock coursing through me. Mia glanced at River, who nodded in return. "A week, at best? We need to make a decision on the best route to proceed here."

"How would we even get her out? Would you have to go into my mind?" I asked, leaning forward. "Not exactly," Mia explained. "But keep in mind, even if we can bring her back into her body, that means you risk never being able to be in control again. Or worse." I took a deep breath in, this is what I signed up for.

But I couldn't help the small voice in my head wondering if I was making a huge mistake. "That's... that's not exactly reassuring." Mia sighed, then squeezed my hand. "Well, it's a complicated situation. But we have the strongest magic here. We can find a solution.

"In the meantime, you'll have a room to stay in and can get to know us." She paused, her tone becoming serious again. "I would advise not to leave the coven. We know you left Xander, and he's looking for you. We've had scouts following him since your arrival." A lump formed in my throat. "I'm so sorry. I didn't mean for any of this to happen. If there's anything I can do to help, I—."

Mia nodded curtly, cutting me off. "Don't worry; we'll figure it out. You can help by staying here and relaxing. It's not going to do us any good if you stress out. And who knows what that could cause for Emma?" I nodded slowly, my mind racing with all the implications. "Kael will be at your side most of the time for safety concerns, just until we figure things out," River added, giving Mia a pointed look that spoke volumes.

"Is there anything else I can do right now?" I asked, searching for a way to contribute. Mia shook her head. "I don't think so. We'll let you know when we figure out what options would be best."

At that moment, the door swung open, and Kael stepped inside. "Are we all done here?"

"Hey, I was just finishing up. She's all yours," Mia smiled, waving goodbye. I braced myself and followed him out into the hallway, which felt like stepping into a new phase of my life. "Well, now that you're caught up, how about we get some grub?" I nodded and followed behind him, still lost in thought. I couldn't believe all of this was happening. The entire day had been one shocking revelation after another.

We walked down the long hallway again, turning down another corridor, and entered a large, open dining hall. The space was enormous, with vaulted ceilings stretching high above, and windows that soared from floor to ceiling, offering a stunning view of the garden and what looked like a market.

Several long wooden tables filled the room, where coven members chatted animatedly or gathered at buffet-style tables, selecting whatever food they liked. My stomach growled loudly, a clear reminder of how hungry I really was. With a grin, I followed him to the buffet, eagerly piling my plate high with pizza, salad, pickled okra, and cottage cheese. As I balanced the towering mountain of food, I noticed Kael stealing a glance at my plate before turning to me.

"What?" I asked, suddenly feeling a bit self-conscious under his scrutiny. He just grinned and shook his head, clearly amused. "Nothing, you just have an interesting taste in food."

My gaze flicked to his plate, which was stacked with orange chicken, rice, and brownies. I couldn't help but laugh. "You're one to talk." He feigned innocence. "Hey, you know what they say—opposites attract," he teased, leading me to a table near the windows, offering a view of the beautiful garden outside.

As I sat down, I took in the faces of the coven members. One man, with dark eyes and black hair, was staring right at me, his expression unreadable. "Who's that?" I asked quietly, eyeing the man warily. "That's Dominick, The Tower. His element is fire, and he doesn't like anyone. He's powerful, chaotic, and a total dick. So, stay out of his way."

I nodded, watching as he stood up with his plate and walked away. "Got it." Scanning the room further, I noticed a girl with long silvery-white hair and striking lavender eyes. Her presence was magnetic, radiating power. "And her?"

"Oh, that's Cassie. The Death card. She's the oldest member and the most powerful, even though she looks like a teenager, wears baggy clothes, and is quiet. She's a total badass," Kael explained. I smiled, digging into my food. The pizza was the best I had ever tasted, and the freshness of the salad was bursting with flavor. "I take it you're enjoying the food," Kael chuckled.

"I don't think I've ever had pizza this good. It's incredible," I replied, genuinely thrilled. He nodded in agreement. "The food here is enhanced by magic; it's all organic and fresh."

"Wow, seriously? The coven must have a lot of power, then," I commented. He nodded. "Yep, they do. We're not the biggest coven, but we have the strongest magic in the realm."

"The realm?" I asked, furrowing my brow.

"You really weren't taught much, were you?" I stared down at my plate, shame washing over me. If I would have stayed with my grandmother, I probably would have known everything there is to know. "No, I guess I really don't."

"There's four realms, including this one. There's the celestial realm and coven. Then there's the Underworld, where only the dead are supposed to go. But they have a strong coven that resides within and then the Shadow Realm, where monsters and shifters reside, although some of the shifters are witches too. I've never been to the Shadow Realm, though.

We have a few allies who live there, but they usually come here or meet us on neutral ground. I've seen pictures, and it's pretty cool." I took a big bite of my okra, trying to wrap my mind around everything he just told me. "That's insane."

"Yeah, I guess it is. So, you really enjoy eating that stuff?" he asked, wrinkling his nose. "Yes, it's an acquired taste. But it's good." He visibly shivered, making a face. "Gross, they're slimy green sticks of doom." I couldn't help but smirk. "You know, for someone who's supposed to be my guardian, you sure are a big baby."

"Hey, I'm still a man," he joked, attempting to regain some dignity. "Those things are just evil." I chuckled, shaking my head. "Sure." Glancing out the window, I noticed the sun beginning to set, casting a blood—orange glow over the sky. The beauty of it all was breathtaking, and I had never experienced anything quite like this before.

"We should get you back to your room. I'm sure you have a big day tomorrow," Kael suggested, breaking the moment. I nodded, standing up and walking alongside him down the hallway. I was amazed at the sheer size of the coven house and its intricate layout.

As we approached my bedroom, Kael suddenly paused, his gaze fixed intently on a point down the hall. "What's wrong?" I asked, sensing the tension in the air.

"We have company," he replied curtly, his body tense. I followed his gaze and saw Dominick staring back at us, his dark eyes piercing and unsettling. The way he looked at me sent a shiver down my spine.

As he advanced, he spoke in a low, steady voice, "I sensed you the moment you entered our sacred grounds, filling it with your darkness. You have no place here. And I will see you pay for what you've done."

His words hit me like a physical blow. My darkness, my past mistakes—they were like a heavy weight pressing down on my chest, and I knew he could feel it. Kael stepped in front of me, trying to diffuse the tension. "Calm down, Dom. We're handling this." But Dominick shook his head, his gaze never leaving mine. "No. This has gone on long enough. She's dangerous, and doesn't belong here."

"Look, I'm not here to cause any problems. I just want to save my friend," Dominick scoffed, his expression hardening as he began chanting. "By the tempest's breath and the storm's own might, may all that is hidden be thrust into light. Shatter the walls that protect your deceit. Let chaos reign where falsehoods meet."

The air crackled with energy, swirling violently around us, sending tapestries flying and doors slamming open. I cried out, trying to shield myself from the storm. I could hardly breathe as memories pummeled my mind, dragging me under. "You will face your mistakes. And learn from them," Dominick growled. "Or you will never be free." Then, just like that, a bright light surrounded me, releasing me from my own personal hell.

A girl's voice rose from the chaos. "Dominick, you weave chaos. But you forget. I stand as the voice of justice. This is not the way. You're only making things worse, and forcing her to see the past won't change the future. Stand down. Now." I blinked a few times, and the room began to come back into focus. A short young woman was standing in front of me, with medium-length golden hair. Her eyes were like two sapphires, glowing brightly.

Dominick sighed, and the energy dissipated, with the lights dimming as he glared at the girl. "This isn't over." And with that, he walked off.

A Path To Reckoning

Kael glanced at the girl. "Sierra, perfect timing," he said, before looking back at me. Sierra turned over her shoulder. "Thanks." She then directed her attention back to me, holding out her hand. "It's a pleasure to meet you. I'm the Justice card. The balance keeper." My head was still spinning from everything that had just happened, a dull ache pounding insistently behind my eyes. "Sorry about that," Sierra continued, her tone light. "Dominick is a bit intense."

"Yeah I noticed. What exactly was he trying to do?" She leaned in slightly, as if sharing a secret. "Well, he cast a spell on you to make you see all the ways your choices have impacted the people around you. I guess it was his way of showing you what will happen if you choose to use the dark arts again."

"Oh..." My stomach churned as the images of Xander and Emma flashed through my mind. Sierra noticed my distress and held out her hand, revealing a silhouette of an angel blowing a trumpet with the letters 'XX' inscribed above it. "Come on, let's take a walk in the garden. Kael, I'll make sure she gets to her room if you want to do your own thing." He looked between us. And after a moment, he nodded. "Okay. Be safe, Lillith."

"Lilly. Just Lilly, please," I corrected him. He smiled in understanding. "Alright, goodnight, Lilly." With that, he turned and headed down the hall, disappearing from view and leaving me with a mixture of relief and apprehension. Sierra turned back to me, concern etched in her features. "Are you okay? Do you want to sit down for a while or something?"

I nodded, feeling the heaviness of Dominick's spell settling deeper within me.

"Please." She led me into the garden, where the air was thick with the sweet scent of blooming flowers, and the rhythmic sound of crickets. It was almost surreal. She guided me to a stone bench nestled beside a gently bubbling fountain. As I sat, I felt my whole body sink into the cool stone.

I understood Dominick's anger and his pain, even if it was hard not to take it personally. The shadows of my past loomed, a constant reminder of the terrible things I had done and the choices I made. Sierra seemed to sense my struggle and sat beside me, allowing a moment of quiet reflection. "You know, facing your demons isn't easy, but it can be liberating," she said gently.

I took a deep breath, letting her words sink in. "I've hurt people, and I've never really apologized for it. Maybe it's time for me to confront that darkness I've been running from." My thoughts drifted back to Emma, the guilt settling like a stone in my heart.

I was trying to make things right, at least with her. The journey ahead wouldn't be easy, but perhaps it was a journey worth taking. I took a deep breath, letting fresh air fill my lungs as the soothing burbling from the fountain nearby calmed my nerves. I'd never felt so out of control in my life. For centuries, I'd been able to manipulate the world around me, shaping it to my will. But now? Now those demons kept coming for me in fresh, terrifying forms.

Closing my eyes, I leaned back against the bench, feeling a gentle breeze dance around me while the sweet scent of lavender filled my senses. I could feel the weight of the moment, the weight of my thoughts, and soon I sensed Sierra sit down beside me. "Hey," she said softly, "are you okay? I nodded, hesitant to open my eyes just yet.

"Yeah. Just a lot on my mind." She was quiet for a moment, and I could almost hear the gears turning in her head. "Listen," she began, breaking the silence, "I know we don't really know each other, but you're safe here. We'll figure this out, I promise."

I opened my eyes and glanced over at her. "Why are you being so nice to me? I don't deserve it. Hell, you're Justice after all. Shouldn't you hate me too?"

She let out a light laugh. "Well, technically, the Justice card represents balance. And balance is important. I also believe that everyone deserves a second chance. You've clearly been through a lot. Besides, it's not like you're the first witch to teeter on the dark side for a bit. And you won't be the last."

"Yeah, but..."

"Listen," she interrupted. "If you were a lost cause, Cassie would have already taken you out. So trust me. You're fine. We'll help you. And we'll figure out what happened to Emma and how to help her. I promise." I nodded, comforted by her words. "Thanks. I appreciate it. And... I'm sorry about earlier. With Dominick. That was a bit awkward." She chuckled.

"Honestly, that was pretty mild compared to what's normal around here. Not everyone gets along. There are seventy-six members. It's a lot of personalities and elements mixing, and it tends to lead to some drama." I laughed, nodding in agreement. "I'm guessing you all are like best friends, though?"

Sierra beamed, her eyes sparkling with mirth. "Most of us, yes. Some of the minor arcana are a bit more standoffish. They don't live here like the others do, but most of us are close. We have to be. We're family."

I chuckled. "Wow. I'm kind of jealous. I wish I had that kind of connection."

"Well, you're here now, right? And your mother found peace here during her time. She even stayed in the very room you do now."

"Wait, really? How do you know that?" She leaned back with a knowing smile. "Because I'm not as young as I look." She winked.

"You were alive during my mother's time? How old are you?"

"Let's just say I've been around for a while. I've seen a lot. The witches here age slower than people outside of the coven."

"So, I still look young, but in reality, I'm a lot older. Like, ancient. Cassie is the oldest, and she's like... a million."

"How could you manage that? Immortality doesn't exist. That's why Xander and I did the soul eater curse, to keep living despite all the terrible things we did for it." Sierra shook her head, her expression turning serious.

"That's not how it works, not exactly. We aren't immortal, not like vampires or angels. We age slower, like shifters do. It's our connected magic that allows us to age slowly and live a bit longer, but eventually, our time comes. And our card signs get passed down to the next worthy witch. No one outside of the coven has this knowledge."

"Wow. So my mom, how did she..." My throat closed up, the question I had long kept at bay surfaced but brought a lump with it—an answer I had never been able to ask before. Sierra's expression shifted, her eyes clouding with sorrow. "It was a dark night. The moon was full, and there was a terrible storm raging. I'd never seen the world so angry and sad all at the same time. I'm not sure what happened, but I was called to the site."

"Your mother was already dead. But you were alive. Screaming. And you were so tiny. A newborn. So, I took you to your grandmother and left you with her." I closed my eyes, tears filling them to the brim. All this time, I'd ached to know the truth about what happened to her and why I was left behind.

Now, as reality crashed down on me, it hurt worse than anything I'd ever experienced. "Thank you for telling me the truth," I managed to say. She nodded, her expression sincere. "Of course. It's what she would have wanted. I can sense it."

A heavy silence fell between us, and eventually I whispered, "I think, I'm ready to go to sleep now. It's been a long day."

"That's a good idea," she replied, quickly getting up. "I'll walk you back to your room." I stood, my legs feeling shaky beneath me as I followed her inside and into the hall. As we passed the main sitting room, I couldn't help but glance inside.

There, a man with long, light blue hair sat with his back to us, a book in one hand and a glass of wine in the other. His aura radiates warmth and power, making me feel oddly comforted. Suddenly, he turned his head, and I gasped as two glowing silver eyes locked onto mine..

His lips quirked up into a casual smile, and just as quickly, he returned his focus to the book. "That's Niko," Sierra said, gesturing toward the man. "The Hanged Man. He's a water user and very intuitive. If you need advice, he's your guy."

"Oh, I see." We approached my bedroom door. And upon arriving, Sierra paused. "Get some rest. We'll talk more tomorrow, okay?" I nodded. "Thanks again for everything."

"Of course. Goodnight," she replied before turning and walking down the hall, her figure disappearing into the shadows. I pushed open my door and stepped in, the quiet comforting me. As I closed the door behind me and sank down onto the bed, worry clawed at my thoughts.

What would happen if we failed to help Emma? It was a terrifying notion that I struggled to shake off. The fear wormed its way into my mind, but I knew I had to confront it. This wasn't just my life or body. I had already lived twenty full lives in the skin of others—each time a parasite slowly killing off their souls.

That's what I was... a parasite... I whispered to myself, with a tear rolling down my cheek. I really had messed everything up, hadn't I? Falling onto the bed, my heart ached with regret. I knew I couldn't undo the past, even though it felt like someone was ripping me apart. A part of this torment was thanks to Dominick's spell, but still, he was right. I deserved to face this.

With each tear that fell, I hoped they would cleanse away some of the darkness gnawing at me. As I lay there, exhausted and overwhelmed by my emotions, I couldn't help but wonder if I could ever truly make things right again.

The Inverted Spell

L illith and Xander had lived full lives—chaos, love, darkness, you name it. But today seemed different. It was a new beginning, a fresh chapter in their wild saga. They were on the hunt, searching for suitable hosts to transfer into—the first lives they would claim and obliterate.

As I glanced around the cozy café, a flicker of nerves rippled through me. It was an unsettling feeling, like a quiet storm brewing just beneath the surface. But then I caught a glimpse of Xander standing steadily beside me, his presence offering a sense of comfort.

"Look at that girl over there," he said, suddenly gesturing toward a petite blonde in the back corner, swirling her coffee cup as if lost in thought. She was undeniably beautiful, with a delicate charm, but there was something deeper lurking beneath—a sadness that clung to her like a second skin.

"She looks a little down, huh?" I murmured, lowering my voice as I studied her features, trying to peel back the layers. "Exactly," he replied, his tone cool and collected, as though he had already mapped out a plan. "That's why she's perfect. She won't put up much of a fight when we make the switch." I swallowed hard, a sense of unease settling in my stomach. The magnitude of what we were considering was heavy

"Okay, but what about her family? Her friends? Don't you think they'll notice something's off?" Xander remained unfazed, his focus locked on the girl. "Think about it. People are so wrapped up in their own lives. They'll assume whatever changes happen would stem from her own drama. Plus, she looks so detached. She'll be easy to slip into."

A shiver ran down my spine at the thought of manipulating her existence. "Easy doesn't mean right," I countered, feeling the weight of my moral conundrum. "Maybe think of it this way," he suggested, shifting his perspective as he glanced at me with his charming grin.

"It's not about destroying her life. It's about giving her a fresh start—a chance to feel something new." Reluctantly, I looked at the girl once more. I weighed my options, but after a moment, I conceded. "Fine," I sighed, the gravity of my decision settling over me like a dense fog. "But we need to be careful. Let's not cause any unnecessary pain."

"Exactly. Now, do you want to help me pick a host?" I felt a spark of adrenaline and nodded. "Yeah, okay." Xander flashed a grin before his gaze began sweeping the café, assessing his options. After a moment's deliberation, his eyes landed on a tall, muscular man in a suit. He was in his early twenties, with dark hair and sharp features that radiated a certain confidence. "That guy over there looks like he's got some real power."

"I agree," I said, tapping my chin thoughtfully as I examined the man. But then I hesitated, uncertainty creeping back in. "But..."

"Don't start. This is what we agreed on," he interrupted quickly, cutting off my internal debate.

"You're taking the girl, and I'm taking the guy."

"Right," I sighed, trying to push back the nagging doubts. "So we approach them, enthrall them, and then take them back to the hotel?" Xander nodded, his eyes sharp and focused on his target. "Perfect. Now go get her. We've got a new life to live."

With a deep breath to steady my nerves, I walked across the café, weaving my way through clusters of tables and patrons. My magic festered beneath the surface, ready to be unleashed as I stepped closer to the girl.

Upon reaching her, I lightly trailed my fingers down her arm, channeling my magic into her, though she remained blissfully unaware of the change on the horizon.

"Hey there," I purred, flashing her my best smile, hoping to draw her into my orbit. "Mind if I sit?" She blinked at me, clearly dazed by both my presence and the unexpected charge in the air. "Yeah, of course."

"Awesome," I said, settling down across from her. "You look like you're having a rough day." At this, she snorted, shaking her head. "That's an understatement. It's been pretty crap lately."

"I'm sorry to hear that," I replied softly, leaning in just a bit more. "I've been in a funk too. How about we help each other out?" Her eyebrow lifted in curiosity, a flicker of interest crossing her features. "What do you mean?"

"Well," I began, trying to keep my tone light and enticing, "I'm staying at a hotel nearby, and I could use some good company. We could vent about our problems over a drink or two. And who knows? Maybe we'll find some magic in the chaos."

She seemed to think it over, biting her lip as the weight of my invitation settled between us. "Okay, I could use a drink. Honestly, things have been pretty awful." I beamed, the excitement bubbling within me like a fizzy drink about to overflow.

My magic was a euphoric high, making people feel good and thoroughly open to 'suggestions'.

"That's the spirit, let's go." I extended my hand, and she took it, a small smile breaking through her initial discomfort. She stood, wobbling slightly as her eyes glazed over with a telltale haze. "Okay, let's do this."

We strolled out of the café, and in the distance, I spotted Xander, already having his chosen host enthralled. Back at the hotel, I had a bottle of wine chilling, ready to set the mood for our newfound companionship.

As soon as we entered the room, the girl made a beeline for the wine, clearly needing a drink after her rough day. I couldn't blame her, and relief was about to come, though it wasn't in the way she expected.

She took a long gulp, her shoulders visibly relaxing as the tension bled away. "This is just what I needed," she sighed, an easy smile spreading across her face.

"Cheers to that," I chimed in, settling down beside her. Moments later, Xander and his host walked in, and he shot me a quick nod, confirming that the man was under his spell. A twinge of fear coursed through me at the thought of what we were about to do, but I quickly pushed it aside. I couldn't let fear rule over me. "So," I said, shifting my focus back to the girl, "tell me about your life. I want to know everything."

She paused for a heartbeat, her brain clearly weighing what she should say. But then, like a dam bursting open, she launched into her story, pouring out details. I needed to grasp every nuance of her life—the highs, the lows, everything in between. It was risky, I knew that, but I needed to do this.For hours, we shared stories and sipped wine, laughter stirring between us.

Time slipped through our fingers, and as the night wore on, I noticed her fight against sleep growing weaker. Her eyelids fluttered as the intoxicating blend of wine and magic gently began lulling her into a dreamlike state.

With a mix of nerves and adrenaline, I took a deep breath and reached out, tentatively placing my hand lightly on her forehead. Instantly, my magic surged up to meet my command.

Just as I was about to make that leap, an unexpected blinding white light exploded around us, washing over the room like a new dawn. "Emma!" someone called, their voice cutting through the haze. Wait, that's me?

Confusion twisted inside me, and suddenly, everything around me dissolved. I was floating into an abyss of unknowns, the world slipping into darkness around me. The laughter and clinking of wine glasses faded, replaced by a profound silence that felt both liberating and terrifying.

I was untethered, suspended between realities, and in that moment, it was as if time had forgotten me. I couldn't tell if I was ascending or descending. As thoughts swirled through my mind, I was acutely aware of a pulsing energy surrounding me, an echo of magic reverberating in the void. And then, just when I thought it couldn't get weirder, fragments of memories and faces flashed before me, each one pulling at the strings of my consciousness. The thrill of magic faded into a heartbeat of uncertainty, and I braced myself for whatever awaited me on the other side.

Lilly

When I woke up, my mind was clear, but my heart was still heavy with the remnants of last night's chaos. The events played on a cruel loop in my head—Dominick's anger, the spell, and the jagged memories that haunted me. With a sigh, I pushed myself out of bed and stretched, feeling my muscles strain and shift as I did. As I shuffled toward the bathroom, a soft knock at the door caught my attention. "Coming." I called out, padding across the room.

I opened the door to find a new face staring back at me. She had midnight blue hair that cascaded like waves, and her eyes reminded me of an embered honey, warm and fierce. "Hi. Can I help you?" I asked, tilting my head in curiosity. She smiled. "Hey, I'm Nyx. The Moon card," she announced, casually holding up her arm to showcase her intricate crescent tattoo surrounded by waves, with the number 'XVIII,' elegantly inked above.

"I know Kael is supposed to be keeping watch, but I figured you'd prefer a woman. So, I'm here to hang with you today. Oh, and I brought you some clothes. I hope they're okay." She extended a bundle of clothing toward me—a simple black sweater and ripped jeans.

I took them, my smile widening. "Thank you. That's really nice of you. Do you want to come in? I just need to take a shower and get dressed, then we can go?"

Nyx nodded and stepped inside, her demeanor kind and almost shy as she glanced around the room, taking in the space I called my own. I headed to the bathroom and closed the door, setting the clothes on the sink before starting the shower. As the hot water cascaded down, I sighed, letting the steam envelop me.

Everything was beginning to be overwhelming—like a tidal wave crashing over me. The constant presence of a stranger, the flood of memories, and the magnitude of the unknown loomed heavily in the air. I wished there was a roadmap for dealing with it all, but I was navigating blindly.

After finishing my shower, I dressed quickly, slipping into the comfortable outfit Nyx had chosen for me. When I stepped out of the bathroom, I found Nyx sitting on the edge of the bed, flipping through a magazine. She looked up, smiling.

"Hey! You look great." I glanced down, feeling a small rush of appreciation. "Thanks! This was really sweet of you."

"Of course. Now, come on, let's go grab some breakfast. I'm starving," I followed Nyx down the hallway and into the dining room, my eyes widening at the spread laid out.

The table was filled with omelets, pancakes, fresh fruits, and parfaits, each dish looking more tempting than the last. Beside it sat a large coffee pot and a pitcher of juice, a delicious feast fit for a gathering. "Wow. you guys sure take breakfast seriously," I said, my mouth watering. Nyx grinned, clearly enjoying my reaction.

"The kitchen is always open, and the cook is a really sweet lady. So, help yourself." I nodded and grabbed a plate. I loaded it with a spinach, cheese, and mushroom omelet, added a generous heap of fruit, and poured myself a cup of coffee.

Nyx did the same, and after a quick clink of our mugs in a silent toast, we headed back down the hallway. "So, where are we going?"

"Well, the council has requested a meeting," she replied, her tone shifting to something serious. "They want me to attend a meeting? Why?" I couldn't hide the skepticism in my voice. Nyx stopped and turned to face me. "Because they might have figured out a ritual that will help, but they need your consent first."

"Wait, seriously?" My heart raced at the thought of a possible solution. "Yes. Now, let's go." I followed her down the hall and up a spiraling staircase. We stopped at the first door to the right, and Nyx knocked. A voice from inside called out, "Enter." She opened the door and led me inside.

The room was imposing, dominated by a long, dark wooden table set in the middle, surrounded by several chairs. At the far end, a podium stood, reminiscent of something you'd see in a courtroom. Cassie stood beside it, flipping through some papers, while Alistair, Bram, and River sat at the table, chatting quietly.

As Nyx and I entered, they all turned their attention to us. "Ah, you've arrived. Have a seat, please," Alistair motioned toward the empty chairs at the end of the table. I obeyed, my hands trembling slightly as I settled into my seat. Cassie cleared her throat, setting a serious tone for the discussion.

"As we discussed yesterday, the council has been searching for a way to help Ms. Cross. And now, we think we've come up with a solution. There's a spell called the Fulcrum of Souls. It should allow us to pull Emma back from wherever she is and put her back in control of her body."

I sat there in stunned silence, uncertainty flooding my mind. It felt too good to be true. "But... how? Is it dangerous?" I asked tentatively. "Well, we have the power." Alistair chimed in, "the fulcrum is a fairly complicated ritual, but it's not without risks. There might be memory overlap or other detrimental side effects. However, it's worth a shot, don't you think?" I nodded slowly, the gravity of the situation sinking in. "Yes. Of course. When can we do this?" Alistair and Bram exchanged a glance.

"Tonight would be our best bet. I know it's short notice, but the sooner we pull Emma out of where she is, the safer she'll be."

"Okay, what can I do?" I asked, eager to contribute. "Just show up," River said, a slight smirk gracing her lips. "Okay, I can do that." Their confidence reassured me as Alistair clapped his hands together. Bringing everyone's attention back to him. "Alright. It's settled then. We'll meet tonight at midnight. Don't be late." With that, I stood up, and the rest of the room followed suit. We began to file out, each of us lost in our own thoughts. However, Kael sidled up beside me, his warm smile anchoring me in the chaos.

"Hey," he said, and I couldn't help but feel a little comforted by his calm demeanor. "Hi, Kael." I shifted on my feet as his eyes seemed to assess me. "How are you holding up?"

"Honestly? Not great." I ran a hand through my hair, feeling the weight of everything. "Emma gets her body back, and I get to go back into the shadows of her mind. I mean, of course, it's what I deserve. It's just scary not knowing what the future holds or if I'll even have one."

He nodded, his expression softening. "It's gonna be alright. There's no way we'd leave you in the void. Especially now that we know there's another soul in there. You know that, right? We will do everything to figure out how to get you a body of your own. Not stolen or anything like that. I promise."

I looked up at him, seeing the sincerity in his gaze, but my defenses rose up. "I don't need false promises. Or lies. I'm a big girl, and I can handle the truth." He shook his head emphatically, stopping to meet my eyes directly. "I wouldn't lie to you. I swear on my life, we will figure out something for you. So you're not just a voice in Emma's head."

"Okay, then I'll believe you. But if you're wrong, you'll be the one to suffer my pranks for the rest of your life," I shot back, a playful edge creeping into my voice. "Deal," he said, extending his hand. I laughed, shaking it firmly. "You're a fool."

"Probably," he replied with a chuckle. "But I'm still a good guy." I nodded, a smile tugging at my lips. "Yeah. That you are." The rest of the day passed quickly, the hours slipping away as the sun began to dip below the horizon.

"Are you ready?" a voice called, pulling me from my thoughts. It was Kael again, breaking into my contemplation. "Yeah, I'm coming," I replied as I pushed myself off the bed. We made our way to the ritual room in comfortable silence, though my nerves propelled me forward with every step.

When we finally entered, the air shifted dramatically. I was greeted by the rest of the coven, all the members standing in a circle, their presence both intimidating and comforting. The 22 leaders stood firmly on the very line, exuding an air of authority

A circle of candles flickered around us, their flames casting dancing shadows against the walls. Various crystals and herbs were arranged carefully, forming a pentagram that pulsed with energy. In the middle of it all was a stone altar draped in a black cloth.

Kael remained by my side, but he was also positioned near another man, a figure I hadn't yet seen before. He stood out immediately, adorned with a striking tattoo of a wheel, a sphinx perched atop and a devil lurking below, with the number X inscribed above it.

Kael motioned for me to come closer, and I obeyed. "This is Lennox, The Wheel," Kael said. "We will be initiating the ritual tonight."

"Hello," I said, giving him a nod, trying to mirror Kael's confidence. "Welcome," Lennox replied. "Are you ready to begin?" I took a deep breath, attempting to ignore the flutter of nerves that had settled in my stomach. "Yeah, I think so." Kael took a step forward. "You're going to be fine. Just stand there and look pretty." He winked at me, with a playful glimmer in his eye, and I couldn't help but grin back.

"Thanks," I replied, feeling a rush of warmth that eased some of my nerves. "Okay, let's do this." Lennox nodded, and without hesitation, he began to chant. His voice started as a low murmur, "We call upon the elements of earth, air, fire, and water."

The moment he spoke, the candles in the room flickered to life, their flames dancing as if responding to his words. The crystals also began to glow with energy, humming with a newfound potency, the energy shifting in the room like a surfacing tide.

As Lennox's voice grew stronger, he invoked the spirit of Hecate, goddess of magic and the moon, "to guide us through this ritual. Let the veil between realms be lifted." With each word he spoke, the candles burned brighter, and the crystals pulsed.

I was falling deeper into an almost trance-like state as he continued. "As it once was, so it shall be. At this moment, I seek a reprieve. With a heart that seeks to mend. "I gather strength to help and defend. By the light of dawn, by the moon's soft grace, I plead for balance in this sacred space. Emma. Arise from shadows deep. Awaken your strength, for it's your power to keep. With every breath, let your spirit soar. Release the chains that bind you no more."

His words echoed within me, and suddenly, there was a sensation akin to weightlessness. My head seemed to droop, and an invisible hand began pulling at my very core, tugging me upward like I was a balloon floating into the sky. No. It wasn't just me—every person in the room was levitating, our feet slowly lifting off the ground.

I struggled to grasp the enormity of what was happening—the chanting, the energy building in the air, and the raw power of the ritual—it all became a blur. "Emma!" I shouted, the sound of my voice swallowed by the chaos. Panic surged, escalating with that all-too-familiar feeling of being yanked apart.

"We can't hold it together! The magic's too strong!" Kael's voice cut through the storm of energy, distant and strained, as if he were shouting from an entirely different planet. I could see him wobbling, struggling to stay grounded in this wild chaos.

His magic flickered like a dying flame as he fought against us, while the others clung tighter to the ritual, embodying a desperation that hung thick in the air. "Focus!" Lennox barked, his voice radiating authority and determination, but Kael's hesitance rippled through the group, sparking hints of doubt.

Concerned glances flitted between us, and I could practically feel the anxiety crackling like static electricity. Then it hit me—another sharp tug against my soul, as if the energy itself were trying to tear me apart. Everything around me spun dangerously, like I was caught in some cosmic blender. I sensed Emma's soul clinging to me, frantically and desperately reaching for stability.

Just when it seemed like chaos would win, a violent snap surged through the air, causing the ritual to spiral completely out of control. In an instant, the coven was thrown back, their collective gasps echoing around us as they hit the hard floor. "Emma, stay with me!" I yelled, my voice slicing through the electrified haze hanging heavily in the room.

Her soul flickered next to mine, a dying light that sent a jolt of fear coursing through me. Then we crashed together, back to reality. For a fleeting moment, everything was still suspended in the aftermath of chaotic energies. But just like that, the candles extinguished, plunging the room into darkness.

I only heard our ragged breaths, the once-thrumming energy now replaced with an eerie silence.

Struggling to sit up, I was heavy and drained, an unsettling sensation washing over me. Something was definitely off—I shouldn't still be in control of Emma's body.

"Emma?" I called out, my voice shaky. "Are you there?"

"Lilly?" Emma rushed into my mind like a bullet, panic dripping from her tone. "SHIT! What's happening?"

"We have a problem," I replied, my throat tight as I tried to grasp the situation. "Like, a big problem."

Through Unfamiliar Eyes

Emma

The room was spinning, and my head felt as if it had taken a solid hit from a sledgehammer. What the hell? I blinked rapidly, trying to adjust to what was happening. *Lilly? What's going on?* My voice came through, high-pitched and panicky. "We have a problem. Like, a big problem," Lilly's voice echoed in my mind, laced with anxiety.

What do you mean, a big problem? I glanced around at the people in flowing robes surrounding us, their expressions a mix of confusion and concern, as dread washed over me. The tall man with dark hair and piercing blue eyes stepped forward. "Who are you?" he asked, his voice steady yet probing. Before I was able to respond, Lilly chimed in.

"I'm Lilly. Emma is trapped inside my head." The man's brow furrowed. "Crap," he muttered. *Where in the hell are we?* I demanded. *The last thing I remember, I was in your memories. Living your life.* The tall man rubbed his temples, trying to regain his composure.

"Lilly, Emma, even though the ritual didn't go as planned, don't worry. "At least this way, Emma isn't at risk of perishing. We can make this work, but it'll take some time. You will both have to be patient."

Patient? I echoed incredulously. *How can I be patient? I just want to go home to my cabin.* Lilly sighed, the weight of guilt palpable in her voice. "Emma... I'm so sorry. The whole thing was a ruse. I didn't realize how much you meant to me as a friend until it was too late. I came here thinking I'd be able to fix what I've done."

My mind churned with anger and hurt. *So, I'm just stuck here?* I asked, my voice trembling. *And what about Alex? Where is he?* A heavy silence settled before Lilly spoke again softly, "Alex is gone. Xander...

he's not the type to show mercy." The words hit me like a punch to the gut, suddenly, I felt a chill race through me.

"Emma, I'm so sorry. I'll explain everything. Just give me a chance." I took a deep breath, trying to steady the chaos in my mind. *Okay,* I replied softly. *I need to know what happened.*

Lilly

Five hours had passed since I laid bare every horrible moment since I had taken over Emma's body. She had stayed quiet the entire time, absorbing my every word like a sponge soaking up water. Yet, I knew there was betrayal simmering beneath her calm facade.

A silent storm brewing. If she hadn't hated me before, she certainly did now. Who wouldn't? "Emma? Do you want to take a tour of the coven?" I asked, trying to lighten the mood. "I'm sure Kael wouldn't mind escorting us."

Yeah, I guess, she murmured barely above a whisper, the weight of her thoughts hanging heavily in the air. Kael stood just outside the door, arms crossed. I forced a smile and waved him in. "Hey, Kael? Would you be up for giving us a tour?"

He shrugged, a slight grin flickering on his lips as if he was used to my impulsive requests. "Sure, why not?" As we moved to leave, I caught a glimpse of Emma's weary expression within my mind, and it twisted my heart. "Em? Are you okay?" I asked softly.

Would you be okay if everything you owned burned, and your life had been at risk for the past week? She snapped, her words sharp and piercing.

"No, I wouldn't. But I feel terrible about what happened, and I swear I'm going to make this right." Emma sighed, her tone softening. *Look, I get it. I mean, I've practically lived your life. The magic felt amazing. And Xander was like the devil on your shoulder, urging you to keep going. I don't blame you. I blame Xander for everything that happened, and I think you should, too.*

I nodded, swallowing hard at the memory. The ache of loss over his absence gnawed at my chest. "I do. That's why I left him." Just then, Kael cleared his throat, breaking into our moment of vulnerability like a sudden gust of wind. "I hate to interrupt, but we really need to start the tour."

The guilt washed over me like a wave as I turned away. "Sorry," I mumbled, steeling myself. "I'm ready. Lead the way." As we stepped out of my room, the mood shifted. The winding halls opened up to an expansive marketplace bustling with activity, vibrant colors clashing in a delightful chaos. Emma remained silent, even though she took it all in, soaking up the lively space.

It must be overwhelming to have her entire reality flipped upside down in such a short time, and I hoped it wouldn't hit her too hard. Kael gestured to a nearby stall, with pastries lined up. "Want one?"

I eyed the treat, the scent of blueberries wafting from the small confection, and nodded. "This is amazing," I groaned, my tastebuds dancing with joy. Kael chuckled, shaking his head slightly. "It's pretty good," he agreed, trying to keep his own smile in check. The man beamed at my reaction, his eyes crinkling.

"I'm glad you like it. Enjoy." As we turned to walk away, I heard him chuckle again. "What?" I asked, raising an eyebrow, curious about his amusement. Kael shrugged, his lips twitching with a suppressed grin. "Nothing. It's just, you have a little something on your cheek," he said, pointing playfully to a smudge of sauce. I reached up, wiping the corner of my mouth with my thumb. "Got it."

As we strolled through the coven, Kael pointed out different shops and landmarks while Emma and I made small talk about the food, the people, and the overall vibe of the place. For a moment, I almost forgot about all the chaos that had led us here. But as we walked along, I began to notice snippets of conversation filtering through the crowd.

Some of the people we passed stared at me curiously, while others seemed to be whispering behind their hands. *What's up with them?* Emma asked, concern creeping into her tone. *Are they staring at us?* "I'm not sure," I whispered back, anxiety creeping in. "But they definitely seem to be talking about something."

Kael glanced over, a frown creasing his brow. "Don't worry about them. Some of the members here are just having doubts. They'll come around." Still, my heart sank at his words.

Of course, they would be having doubts—after all, it's not like the ritual worked. For all they knew, I was faking everything. "I don't think they believe me," I murmured. "I mean, look at them. They're staring like I'm some kind of freak." Kael shook his head, trying to reassure me. "They'll get used to you. Just give them some time."

I nodded, though the pit in my stomach didn't go away. As Kael continued the tour, I couldn't shake the feeling that the other coven members didn't trust me. There had to be something to get Emma her body back because then, surely, they'd believe her.

My thoughts drifted back to the ritual we had attempted earlier, the one that had ended in a spectacular disaster. The memory still sent a chill down my spine—yet it had given me a chance to bond with Emma.

I realized she didn't seem to hate me anymore. In fact, I found that we were beginning to become friends. I glanced over at Kael, who seemed lost in his own thoughts as well.

I wondered if I was as disappointed about the outcome of the ritual as I did. I was still struggling with the aftermath, and it was clear Emma was as well.

I wanted to ask him what he thought about the whole thing, but the words died on my lips. I couldn't bring myself to broach the subject—not after everything that had happened. Instead, I followed along as Kael pointed out various sights, trying to force a smile and pretend everything was okay.

But deep down, I knew it wasn't. The doubt and anxiety gnawed at me as we passed through the marketplace. Finally, the tour came to an end, and we headed back to my room. As soon as the door closed behind us, the facade fell away like a mask, and I collapsed on the bed, burying my face in the pillow.

My mind was a whirlwind of how to reverse the mess I'd made. There were no guides for this kind of problem—no books that outlined how to fix situations like ours. *Do you think it will be permanent?* Emma asked softly, her voice breaking through the fog of silence.

I swallowed hard, a lump rising in my throat. "I don't know," I admitted. "I hope not." The quiet stretched between us until Emma finally spoke again. *Can I ask you a question?* There was a hesitation in her tone, and it made my heart flutter uncomfortably. "Sure, what is it?"

What made you leave Xander? In your memories, I sensed his obsession growing slowly—turning into control and all that. But you two were together for two hundred years. I saw the way you looked at each other. Lived it even.

"Xander changed," I began, fiddling with the frayed edge of my blanket. The memories of our past still haunted me, the laughter we'd shared under the stars, but those memories twisted like a knife in my gut. "He became... possessive.

When I finally opened my mouth to express my worries about all the harm we were causing—especially to you — he shut me down.

I loved him, but I couldn't stay locked away in that life anymore, dragging you down with me. I knew I had to leave."

Emma was silent for a moment as she processed my words, her absence of speech almost louder than any response. Then, with a shaky breath, she spoke again. *I'm glad you left him. But what if… what if one day he comes looking for you? Or worse? What if we do get me back in control of my body, and he tries to hurt me?*

"I won't let that happen," I replied, hoping my confidence would reach her. But as her fears crisscrossed my thoughts, I couldn't help but wonder the same thing. *What if he gets his hands on me and hurts me because I'm a mortal? Or because he knows I was in your soft spot?*

Her question hit hard, and I didn't want to think about it. Or the possibility of Xander coming back to ruin everything. I slipped off the bed, pacing the small space of the room as I processed both our fears. "You're right," I said quietly, wishing desperately that she wasn't

Just then, an idea struck me, and I paused mid-step. "What if I were to teach you magic?" Emma's surprise momentarily broke through her anxiety. *Yeah, okay. Now that's insane.* She laughed, but there was an undercurrent of curiosity in her voice.

"Is it?" I countered, my mind racing with possibilities. "How else will you protect yourself when we finally get you back in control? Hide in the coven's realm the entire time? That's not a life anyone would want." *I don't know. That seems impossible. I mean, how would you even know I could do it?* "That's the beauty of magic," I said, waving my hands excitedly.

"You don't need a body or anything to cast spells. Besides, think of it as a chance to have fun. Learning together. What do you say? Wanna give it a shot tomorrow?" She paused, the wheels clearly turning in her mind. *Okay, fine. I'm in.*

"Perfect." I grinned as I flopped back into bed. "Now get some sleep. It's been a long day, and tomorrow we've got some work to do." As the night gradually wore on and the room settled into a blanket of stillness, my eyes grew heavy. I nestled into the comfort of my pillow, and images of what tomorrow might bring swirled through my mind. "Sweet dreams, Em," I murmured.

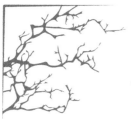

Transcendence

Lilly's Dream

The forest seemed like a dream, with mist swirling around me, clinging to my skin as fireflies danced among the trees that loomed overhead. Their dark bark glinted with an unsettling sheen that caught the faint light, casting shadows that twirled and flickered along the ground.

The air was thick with the scent of damp earth and something else, something ancient and lingering As I wandered deeper along the winding path, the mist thickened, dragging at my ankles and pulling me further in.

Tiny flickers of movement caught my eye in the corners of my vision, hinting at creatures watching me with curiosity, their eyes glistening like drops of dew. But every time I turned, there was nothing there, only the feeling of being observed. Finally, I stumbled into a clearing bathed in silvery moonlight, illuminating a beautifully crafted stone altar at the center.

The altar was etched with strange symbols that pulsed softly in the light, drawing me closer. Curiosity tugged at my instincts, but a whisper of caution told me something wasn't quite right.

Lying on the altar were three tarot cards, each glowing faintly as if they had been waiting for me. I leaned closer, my heart thudding in my chest, and studied the first card. The Hanged Man. It depicted a figure upside down, a calm expression on its face that somehow intrigued me.

The meaning struck me hard—sacrifice and the need to see life from a different angle. A slight unease unfurled in my chest, a twinge that seemed like a warning. With a quick breath, I flipped over the second card. Death. Instinctively, my heart raced, but as I focused, I noticed the vibrant roses framing the skeletal figure.

This wasn't just about endings. It was about transformation. Change often demanded shedding the past to step into something new. Without wasting any time, I turned over the third card. The Lovers. The image captured two figures intertwined, glowing softly—symbols of unity and commitment. Yet the message of choices and balancing desires loomed in my mind. For a moment, I was lost in thought, my mind darting to Emma. The tangled threads of our situation were heavy, as if each choice was either pulling us closer or shoving us apart. Sacrifice, transformation, choices. I had to figure it out—and fast.

I woke up with a start. The cards, the forest, the fates were nudging me towards the answer I sought.

It was clear I had to choose, but which choice? As I contemplated while getting ready for the day, the lingering uncertainty clung to me. My stomach twisted in knots, and I forced myself to take a deep breath to shake off the nerves. Just then, Emma's voice broke through. *Hey, you okay?*

Blinking at the sudden intrusion, I took another breath and replied, "Yeah, just... thinking about everything." I offered her a small smile, hoping to reassure her that I was okay. *I can see why. This whole thing, it's a lot, isn't it? So, are we doing some magic lessons today?*

"Definitely," I replied, glancing around the room as if the walls might have the answers I sought. "Where would be a good spot for that? We'll need privacy." *Well, we could always do it in our room. Or maybe check if the coven has some sort of training room? I bet they'd let us use it.* "Good idea. Let's ask around."

I stepped outside, and Kael, as usual, was waiting by the door, leaning casually against the frame in a way that somehow always put me at ease. "Morning." I greeted him, giving him a playful nudge with my shoulder.

"Morning, Lilly, Emma," he said, a grin spreading across his face, his eyes sparkling mischievously.

"Did you both sleep well?" *Like a log,* Emma quipped. *How about you? Any wild dreams about saving the world?* I couldn't help but echo her question.

"Not this time. Just epic battles with laundry," he replied, laughing. "But anyway, what's on the agenda today?"

"Magic lessons."

"Sweet. I'd love to tag along. Let's see if we can snag the training room. I could use a little magic practice myself."

"Of course," I agreed. "I wouldn't want it any other way." He led us down the long hallway, then turned left, going up a set of spiral stairs. There were a few doors, and he paused at one near the end. Opening the door revealed a large room with a high ceiling, sunlight streaming through the windows, casting a warm glow across the space.

Plush carpet cushioned our steps, and a few comfortable chairs and tables dotted the floor. "This is it," Kael announced, gesturing around him. He looked at me curiously. "What type of magic will you be teaching her?"

"Well, I'm not sure," I admitted. "I thought maybe we'd start with some simple spells and see where that takes us."

"That sounds like a good plan," he agreed, moving to lean against the wall. "I'll stay here and watch over you two, just in case something goes wrong."

"Thanks," I nodded, feeling slightly reassured.

Emma

"Okay, Em, you ready?" *As ready as I'll ever be,* I replied, glancing at the scattered chairs. *What do you want me to do?* "Well, spell-casting

127

is all about intention. We'll start with something simple—my grandmother's cloaking spell to make things invisible. Just repeat after me. You can sing, hum, or say it in your head. Whatever feels natural. Here we go. 'Veil of shadows, soft and deep. Hide my treasures, a secret to keep.'

I took a deep breath, letting the words roll off my tongue, their rhythm soothing and inviting. I repeated the incantation over and over, feeling the surrounding air begin to shift, thickening with an almost electric energy. But just as quickly, it faded away, leaving the room dull once more.

It didn't work, I said, trying to suppress the disappointment creeping into my voice. Lilly nodded, her expression calm. "That's okay. I felt your magic. You have it in you. It just takes practice." Swallowing hard, I took a deep breath to center myself and tried again.

I spoke the words again and again, each time a flicker of something stirring within me. But each time, that spark slipped through my fingers, leaving me frustrated.

Just when I was beginning to be discouraged, Lilly's voice broke through my spiraling thoughts. "Hey, Em?" she said softly, drawing my attention back to her. "Can you try something for me?" *Sure, what is it?*

"I want you to close your eyes and picture yourself on a beach. The sun is shining bright above you. You can feel the warm sand between your toes, and you hear the steady crash of waves against the shore. Can you do that?" I nodded, closing my eyes and allowing myself to sink into the scene she conjured. The sound of the waves seemed to echo in my ears as the warm sun surrounded me.

And I could almost smell the salt in the air. "Good," Lilly continued, her voice low and soothing. "Now, take a deep breath. Inhale slowly, hold it for a moment, and then exhale gently. With each breath, focus on the calm and peace surrounding you. "Let go of any worries or fears, and let the energy flow through you." I followed her instructions meticulously.

My breath steadied—deep, slow, and rhythmic. "Now, repeat the words of the spell," Lilly urged. "But this time, visualize the energy flowing out from your fingertips. Everyone's energy looks different and takes on unique forms. Imagine yours." With my eyes still closed, I began to recite the spell once more. This time, as I spoke the words, I truly felt something shift inside of me.

The air began to shimmer, and tiny sparks of deep purple flickered to life around my hands like fireflies in the dusk. An aura of power swirled within my palm. "That's it, Emma," Lilly encouraged. "You're doing it." The energy swirled around me as if it were a living thing, growing and intensifying with each repetition of the words.

The energy coalesced and surged as if it had a life of its own, climbing up the chair's legs and spreading through the space until it started to fade from sight.

Lilly

My jaw fell open in awe as I watched the chair vanish before my eyes. It remained for a moment, shimmering and warping like a mirage on a desert before it faded completely from view. I saw Emma's magic, a deep purple aura enveloping me.

Just as quickly, it winked out, and the chair appeared again. A stunned, delighted smile spread across my face. But no sound came out as we stared in silence at the chair. "Wow, I knew you could do it, Em." I finally managed. *I wish I could give you a great big hug,* she gushed, her excitement reverberating through me.

The happiness radiating off of her took my breath away. *Thanks Lil, I couldn't have done it without you.* My throat tightened, and it was hard to form words, but I choked out a reply. "It was nothing. Let's keep going. Okay?"

Oh yes, please. We went through a couple more easy spells, successfully casting the glamor spell that made a chair change color and shape. She was a natural. "Are you sure you've never cast a spell before?" I asked, surprised.

Well, I was stuck being you in your memories, so technically I had, but that was an awfully weird experience.

She laughed. And I sighed, leaning into the soft cushions of the chair. "You're a quick study, exactly as I was," I told her. *I remember a couple of the spells your grandmother taught you. She was so supportive until...*she trailed off. *Well, you know.* "Xander." I finished for her as tears began brimming my eyes at how I turned my back on her.

She truly was trying to help me become my best self and go beyond what I had thought of as my limits. And now? She was gone. I'd outlived her due to the Soul Eater's spell. It was devastating.

Love can make people reckless. Emma whispered. "I'd rather be with my grandmother or you than some man, no matter how well it seems to work out," I confessed. *Agreed.* Her sympathy was evident. She lived through it all with me, in a way. It brought me even closer to her.

Once it was clear our lesson for the day was complete, I tucked the book on spell casting away for the next day's lesson. "Kael, show us some of your magic. Please?" A mischievous smile crept across his face. "Well, being the strength card, my powers tend to be more physical than magical." He glanced around, striding over to the chair we'd just finished vanishing. He flexed, the muscles in his arms bulging as he lifted it overhead.

"Okay, tough guy, but even I can lift a chair over my head." I challenged him. "Is that so? Come here and give it a go, then."

Furrowing my brow in concentration, I steeled myself and reached for the chair. Even putting my back into it, it didn't budge. "What is this thing made out of?" I grumbled. He laughed, the deep rumbling sound sending shivers down my spine.

"Regular wood, same as yours," he teased. "Okay, I admit defeat. You're very strong. Satisfied?" His grin widened. "Completely." Huffing, I did my best to fight the blush of embarrassment creeping into my cheeks. Stepping away from him, I started making my way out of the room when something else caught my eye. Sitting on one of the chairs was a book. I picked it up and the title immediately caught my attention.

'**Fate's intervention** By Sorcha Flanagan.'

"What's this doing here?" Kael walked over, brows furrowed as he took the book from my hand, flipping through it. "It's empty," he shrugged. Was he losing his mind? I could see the writing in it plain as day.

I don't see anything either. Emma said. "That can't be right. Someone's clearly been using it as a journal or something. Look, they've filled half the pages." Kael's expression changed, eyes widening with understanding. "There are several books in the library. Some are spelled for a specific person's eyes. It's like fate's way of giving that person a message. Maybe it's meant for you?"

"I guess so. I mean... if nobody can see it except me, yeah?" Tossing the book into the air, he flashed me a brilliant smile as it fell into my outstretched hands. "Definitely meant for you. Maybe you should take some time to look it over."

I nodded, tucking the book under my arm as we made our way back to my bedroom. Once we settled in for the night and were lying in bed, I decided to take Kael's advice and break out the journal, flipping the pages with morbid curiosity.

Shock rippled through me upon seeing the first page. The three tarot cards I saw in my dream were illustrated on it, accompanied by a note at the bottom. 'You must make a sacrifice for the path to be purged. Or something you value deeply will disappear, never to be seen again.'

On the next page was a spell, with a list of ingredients. Bone Dust–Ground from the recently deceased. A Black Candle. Fresh Blood. Nightshade. A Mirror. A Lock of Hair. Salt. Once all are placed properly, you will recite the spell. I read through it, disbelief and dread coursing through me. No, no, it can't be.

There has to be another way. I flipped through the pages of the book in desperate frustration. I saw note carded messages that just seemed to mock me, but finally, on the very last page, was an envelope, my name scrawled across it in elegant penmanship.

Slowly, I opened it, trying to calm the turmoil in my chest.

Dearest Lillith,

You were brought into this world with great potential. But like many times before, your potential went unfulfilled. For this, the entire universe grieves for you. This burden on your shoulders is great, but I have faith you shall succeed. Every end has a new beginning. To fully ascend, you must show your strength. I hope you will find the courage to complete your transformation.

With Fates Grace,

Sorcha

My chest constricted as I closed the book. Now knowing what I have to do to save Emma, but the cost of it was monumental. A price no one should have to pay, but perhaps the punishment fits the crime. I've lived many lives. Over and over again, what right did I have to steal Emma's on top of all of those?

What does it say? Emma's voice filtered through my head. I froze, eyes wide. I couldn't tell her. She'd never allow me to do this, but I have to. And I'd live with the choice I had to make. Tears slipped from my eyes as the weight settled on me. *Lil?* "I'm so tired, I think I just need to try to get some rest for tonight, maybe tomorrow, it will make better sense."

Oh, okay. Can I ask you something? I nodded, my face still in the pillow. "Yes." *What made you choose to take over my body?* "Why do you ask?" *I was wondering.* She began. *You could have chosen anyone, but you chose me.* I took a deep breath. "Call it fate, I guess. But It wasn't my choice really, Xander had told me someone moved into our cabin, someone young, suffering, and that you'd be an easy host to take over."

"But after bonding with you, I actually really enjoyed my time we spent together. And I know I was a huge pain in the butt. Yet, I know you enjoyed me being there, too. Right?" *Yeah, I suppose I did. You always kept me on my toes and moving instead of being swallowed by grief. Thank you.* Tears began sliding down my cheeks, dripping onto the pillow.

"We'll make tomorrow the best day yet. And thank you, Em. We wouldn't be as close as we are now if not for your strength." *Indeed, we wouldn't.* She agreed, the warmth in her tone soothing. "Goodnight Em, and thank you. For everything." *Goodnight Lil.*

Cherished Moments

Lilly

Bright sunlight crept through the window, shining in my eyes. I rolled over, taking a few minutes before I fully emerged from sleep. As usual, my brain sprang to life first. An image of the diary appeared in my mind. The reminder that today could be the day everything changes.

I sat up, and I could tell Em was still deep in slumber. It was morning, but early enough I could get ready for the day and then gather what I needed for the ritual. While also planning for the best day Emma has ever had.

My goal was to make sure this was a day she'd never forget. A small knot twisted in my stomach and tightened. I swallowed down a lump of worry and slid quietly out of bed. After turning on some soft music, I gathered the supplies from the bathroom that I needed to spruce myself up.

While I knew the point of Emma's day wasn't for me to play dress up and obsess over how I looked, I wanted to make sure she looked amazing when she returned to her body. Emma really did have an amazing olive complexion and smooth skin.

Her dark, naturally curly hair would be a lovely contrast against the purple in the outfit. Not to mention, doing these things helped me relax, and there was a ton to be worried about today, in addition to the uncertainty of this path I had to tread.

I layered her makeup to perfection, bringing out her natural beauty, enhancing the curls in her hair, and lining her deep blue eyes with a brilliant purple and black, making her look fierce. With all that done, I stepped out of the bedroom. Instead of Kael, cassie, or river waiting for me.

I was shocked to see long, light blue hair, and startling silver eyes. "Niko, what are you doing here?" His teeth flashed in a wolf-like grin before he gave me a low, graceful bow. "The others are busy. You're stuck with me today. It looks like it's going to be a fun day.

Your essence feels both excited and grieved. "Seems like a strange combination." He eyed me appraisingly, his head tilted in curiosity. My eyes widened, surly he doesn't know? He seemed to gather the answer I was looking for and cleared his throat. "Emma will be fine, Lilly. That being said, we are fate's hands."

He gave me a wink and turned to walk down the hallway, calling over his shoulder. "Today is a beautiful day, let's go have some fun," He sang as he strode out. *Morning Lil, it seems you've started without me.*

"I didn't want to wake you. So, I thought it might be best to let you sleep in. After everything you've been through." I rubbed my arms as anxiety crawled up my spine. *Huh, well thank you. I wonder why the others want us to be babysat?* She asked, confusion clear in her tone.

A titter escaped from my lips. I wasn't quite ready to delve into the fact I'm practically a criminal in their eyes and under any circumstances I wouldn't be allowed to roam freely. "It'll change soon Em, don't worry about it." Niko led me through the hall, and into a part of the coven's house I wasn't familiar with.

I let him lead the way, which led me down several more corridors and then up a few flights of stairs before we wound up back outside in a long open breezeway surrounded by weeping willows. It was beautiful, but deadly. With flowers and vibrant, spiky and green plants.

"Wow, why have I never been to this side of the coven before?" Niko gave a soft chuckle, his shining eyes crinkling around the corners. "This is my domain, per se. I enjoy the energy nature provides and getting away from all the muskiness and heaviness of the archives and library."

Wow, all these different plants are amazing. Emma gushed, giving me a shove forward so she could have a closer look. I made my way over to a shrub with spiny quills sticking out at odd angles and pale pink star-shaped flowers.

"What are these?" I marveled, keeping my distance as I enjoyed the view. "Ah, this is a hedgehog cactus. Perfect for any cacti lover, though some are a little trigger-happy. Best for indoors. The white cactus behind them is Echinocactus grusonii," Niko rubbed his hands together excitedly, going into a ramble.

"Not only do they come in an array of beautiful colors, their blooms are large and last for weeks. They produce a sweet nectar that honey bees simply adore." He gently reached in and plucked one of the yellow spikes. Then, with an elegant gesture, pressed the sharp spike to my lips.

Reluctantly, I closed my eyes and parted my lips. The sharp, almost woody taste was met by a flavorful burst of sweetness across my tongue. *Wow,* Em's voice slid into my head, making me smile. "You can say that again."

Grinning, Niko gestured for me to follow him out of the garden. We spent some time in a forested area, where a beautiful field full of wild flowers and shrubs stretched out before us. For several hours, I was able to put aside my guilt, and let myself enjoy the time I got to spend with both Niko and Emma.

We sat down on a grassy hill, lush with beautiful and fragrant wildflowers, then lay back. Staring up at the azure sky peppered with fluffy white clouds. "You know, everything is going to be okay, right?" Niko mused. I blinked up at him, my throat clenched with emotion. Gazing at him, tears filled my eyes. "How do you know?" I whispered. "It's written in the stars. Just as the cycle of life continues, so shall you."

The gentleness and power in his words were so simple, yet the knot in my stomach tightened, wrenching my chest. I nodded quietly, a single tear sliding out of the corner of my eye. *What are you talking about?* Emma chimed in.

"Just life Em. The way things change, and nothing lasts forever. It's just something we're going to have to accept." I took a deep, trembling breath. "It's true," Niko stated. "But we must cherish every moment as it comes." Agreeing, I gave Niko a slight smirk and willed my apprehension to slide away, at least for the moment.

As night began to fall, I started wringing my hands, a nervous ache fluttering in my chest. "You can do this, it's just a matter of taking the leap, and landing on solid ground," Niko assured.

"Thank you." My words were soft and low, afraid my voice would shatter if I spoke above a whisper. He handed me a bag of ingredients from the pantry. "Guess you haven't explained anything to Em?"

"No, but I was hoping you will be waiting to help her after? For her?" Niko dipped his head in acquiescence. "I'll be there." His reassurance lingered in the evening air as we made our way back toward the coven's house.

The path was now framed by twinkling lanterns that began to fill the courtyard with a warm, golden glow. The enchanting fragrance of night-blooming jasmine wrapped around us. "We should head to the Market before it gets too late," Niko said, his eyes darting toward my face, gauging my mood.

"It's a perfect spot for distractions, and trust me, you'll love the freshly brewed moonberry tea." He grinned. *Moonberry tea? Sounds interesting, I'm down.* Emma chimed in.

We strolled through a garden that buzzed with arcing fireflies. We exited the confines of the coven grounds and stepped into the market square. *Wanna grab a few trinkets?* Emma asked, knowing my penchant for the eccentric.

This time, I was thankful for the distraction. And wandered the narrow street, admiring all the shimmering tents. I bypassed the first few until I spotted an open tent strung with paper lanterns and candle sticks. Its long silk covered tables were riddled with unique items, but my eyes set on the crystals that glimmered and caught the reflection of the flickering candlelight.

"Welcome." An aged, husky voice greeted us. I was surprised to see a wiry old woman sitting behind the counter, her pointed features and silvery robes adding to the long, cascading braids that hugged her shrunken shoulders.

She tilted her sharp chin and blinked her watery blue eyes, waiting. On her wrist was a tattoo of a lantern with the number IX inscribed above. The hermit. She reminded me of every fortune teller, Gypsy, and wiccan elder I'd ever read about. I looked over at the set of crystals.

"Em? Do you see any that you like?" I asked. *Well, they are all so pretty. I wonder what they're for?* I held back a smirk. "Well, point some out. And I'll tell you."

Emma and I picked out a few crystals that she agreed she liked. Then we made our way to the wand shop. I had one of my own, but Emma would need one. We walked down a hallway and into another side street, making my way through more vendors. Turning right, we entered a quiet little shop.

The instant wave of heavy incense and the wafting aroma of aged oaken casks assaulted my nostrils. The scent made me feel lightheaded and more relaxed than I had been in days. A tall, slender man greeted us. He seemed ambitious, with fiery red hair and passionate orange eyes. His tattoo was of a flame atop a wand with the number I.

He must be the Ace of Wands, Caleb. "Hello, looking for a wand? Or perhaps a foci?" His mellow tone glided between us. *A wand!* Emma gushed, practically vibrating with excitement.

I almost choked on a laugh. "Yes, a wand. Emma is going to pick one for herself."

"Follow me to our selection of wands. In this case, you may choose whichever one you like," He grinned. Taking off the glass cover and stepping away. He gestured for Emma to come forward.

"Begin your search." *I think I'd like the wand that's ashy gray, twisted pine, and flecked with white.* "Okay, you got it." I eyed the first couple. The grayish-white wand was close to the back of the case, almost at the bottom row.

I pushed my hand in and pulled out a sleek, stately specimen. And Emma's energy lit up. "We'll take this. It's perfect."

"Great. I'll wrap it up and you'll be good to go." Caleb took the wand and quickly wrapped it. Then handed it back to me. "Thank you."

"Thank you as well. Come back anytime." Niko had stayed by the door, looking over some of the strange mixes of herbs. He perked up when I approached. "Oh? You've found what you're looking for?"

"Yes, we found a wand. Thank you,"

"Now you'll never be left wandering around without protection," he winked. "That's exactly the point." I grinned, hoping his words would carry through to Em. "Is the moonberry tea still available at the outdoor cafe?"

"It is. And we get a spectacular view to go with it." We strolled around a bit, leaving the main part of the market and made our way up a long hill where we sat at a simple, elegant, and quaint tea house nestled within a garden of flowers.

A giant stone hearth dominated the center, and several round tables and chairs encircled it. At the top of the structure, a large mosaic symbol of a fiery bird was etched into the tiles. A sweetly spicy smoke burned in the firepit, making my eyes water.

As we sat down at one of the vacant tables, a tall woman made her way toward us, a long, flowing skirt accentuating her curvaceous figure. Her wavy red curls tumbled down her back. "Welcome to the rising phoenix," she purred in her husky, soothing voice, her eyes the color of emeralds, her skin luminescent in the afternoon sunlight.

Niko perked up, giving the woman a smile. "Hello Violet." Her lips curled into a pleased smile. "Good evening." her eyes darted to me. "What brings you both here?"

"Just some of your famous tea, if you would please?" Niko interrupted.

She gave a soft chime of laughter. "Of course, I'll be right back." Violet came back not a moment later with a steaming clear teapot filled with beautiful herbs and flowers, along with something magical.

After she placed the tray onto our table, she gracefully poured us a large helping of the moonberry tea. My lips curled into a smile, taking in its deep, purplish-black hue that sparked with small, glittering specks in the candlelight. It looked as if the stars themselves swam throughout the dark liquid.

Once it had stopped steaming, I carefully picked up the dainty cup, with the smell of sweet berries mixed with sage, verbena, rosemary, and lavender perfuming the air. I took a sip.

Lilly? Oh. My. Gods. This stuff is delicious, Em growled in delight. My smile stretched as wide as a Cheshire Cat. I almost laughed at her reaction. "It does." I agreed, looking up. Niko's eyes were reflecting the moonlight and the fire in the hearth, making his eyes look molten silver. "The tea really is amazing," he agreed.

The three of us sat in a comfortable silence while we enjoyed the tea. *When are we going to begin that spell?* I couldn't help the sigh that fell from my lips. "When we get back to our room." *Alright, but you seem... hesitant?* It was almost as if she were trying to probe my mind. I couldn't put any of it into words, but I definitely had a twist in my gut.

A moment later, the moonberry tea had begun to relax me and buzz through my veins. Placing my hands on the table, I pulled myself up, ignoring Emma's words. "I'm ready." I whispered.

Threat Of Renewal

A rush of magic washed over me as Lilly whispered goodbye, a frigid wave crashing against my chest. My world tilted and swayed, the air thick with unsaid words and impossible truths. She was leaving. Dying. I didn't know how I knew it. But it was a raw and instinctive realization sinking deep into my gut.

"No!" I yelled out, panic clawing at my throat, but the walls only swallowed my plea. The door swung open, and Niko rushed to my side, the sudden burst of motion pulling me from my spiraling thoughts. "Em, she's gone. I'm so sorry." His words rolled over me like a tidal wave, cold and suffocating.

"What did she do? What's happening?" My voice shook, as if the ground beneath my feet had crumbled away. Niko sighed, a deep crease appearing between his brows that only amplified my dread. "She sacrificed herself so you could have your life back. It was the only way." Panic morphed into a burst of anger at his calm disposition.

"You knew, didn't you?" I accused. My words, sharp and bitter. "You knew this would happen!" My voice rose, the frustration twisting inside me like a coiling serpent. "Why didn't you stop her?"

"Em, you don't understand—" Niko began, but I cut him off, the fury boiling over. "Don't I? I understand you could have done something," I snarled, pushing myself off the bed. Niko stood up, his shoulders squared, and had a stern look in his eyes. He didn't say anything, but I knew he wouldn't have done anything to change this.

The hard truth slammed into me, my anger dissolving into a painful ache in my chest. I slumped back down on the bed, overwhelmed by defeat. In that moment, every time I had taken Lilly for granted, crashed over me in a wave of guilt. I had always assumed she'd be there, in an ever-present light.

But now, faced with the stark reality of her absence, a suffocating panic enveloped me, drowning my thoughts in a rushing flood of fear. Niko stepped closer, reaching out. His fingers grasping my chin and lifting my gaze to meet his silver eyes.

They sparkled with a fierce intensity that compelled me to look closer, drawing me in like a moth to a flame. "Look at me," he urged, his voice low but steady. "I can't... I can't lose her," I finally whispered, each word wrapped in a chokehold of emotion, the tears still simmering beneath the surface, waiting for permission to fall. "It'll be okay. Fate has a way of working miracles. When one thing ends, another begins."

His words were a soft rumble that sent a warm shiver across my skin. "Lilly gave you everything. Including her magic. That star on your wrist? It means you're one of us now—a hand of fate."

My eyes widened, and I glanced down at my wrist and gasped. The familiar birthmark—Lilly's birthmark—had morphed into something more formidable. Under my fingertips, there was a faint pulse, an energy that resonated deep within me, her essence intertwined with mine.

But it was different, charged with an electric undercurrent that thrummed against my skin. Lilly had left me with a part of herself to guide me forward, and the thought made my throat tighten with emotion. I couldn't help the filtering emotions overwhelm me. And bitterness rose again. "I don't want this." I erupted.

"You think I'm going to waltz around like some kind of...of Star just because the fates said so?" He didn't respond. Didn't flinch at my venomous tone, his silver eyes watching me as if he knew I needed to unleash everything churning inside of me. So, I did.

I let out all the grief, the confusion, and the pain. The tears finally began falling. Once I was all cried out, the room fell silent. Niko pulled me closer, wrapping his arms around me and resting his chin on the top of my head. "I wanted more than anything to help her. But this was the only way to get you your life back.

This is what she wanted, Em." I shook my head. "It's not fair." My words were muffled. "How can I be this star? I don't know anything about magic?"

"Neither did she at first, but it came with time. And practice. You were able to cast spells even before you had your body back. And the Star? It symbolizes hope and renewal—a guiding light in times of uncertainty. You might not realize it yet, but you have a destiny, Em. The fates are never wrong."

I searched his face, torn between my rage at him for not stopping Lilly and the reality of what this all meant for me. "So, what does that even mean? What am I supposed to do now?" He shook his head slowly, running a hand through his tousled hair—a gesture that somehow anchored me in the chaos swirling around us. "I don't know, but I suspect you're going to find out."

Xander

Pure rage consumed me, a wildfire igniting deep within my core, as I watched Lillith—a flame I had stoked for centuries—choose that pathetic human over our eternal bond. My Lillith. How had she twisted herself into believing that fleeting mortality was worth more than the eternity we had carved together in the shadows?

My heart cracked as she teleported away, that moment suspended in time—her form flickering out like a dying candle. She was mine, and yet, she had turned her back on the abyss we'd built together. I could still see the look in her eyes as she stood before me, a mixture of fear and defiance as she made her choice.

My beloved had forsaken our bond to save a wretched soul she was meant to destroy. It didn't matter, though. I would claw my way through the darkness to reclaim what was rightfully mine. No one could take her from me—not that human, not that pitiful coven. I would drag her back to me, kicking and screaming, if that was what it took.

She had no idea of the depth of the betrayal, but she would learn. She would learn, and she would regret every unholy decision she made. I let out a primal scream, a sound that ripped through the night like a thunderclap, pulling the stars from their serene slumber. Magic surged around me like a tempest, a dark energy that was uniquely ours. Her precious hideout experienced the wrath of my fury, collapsing in on itself, burning under the weight of my despair and rage—an inferno that reflected the chaos within.

They would suffer for her betrayal. Every person that stood in my way would feel my pain. And once I tore down Mystic Hollow, once it lay in ruins, then I would cleanse myself in the ashes.

I Turned my gaze towards the blazing ruins of her hideaway, a smirk creeping across my lips. Let the world tremble, let them all bear witness to the chains I would forge anew.

Emma

I sat on the edge of the bed, the cool fabric of the sheets crumpled beneath me, staring at my hands as they lay motionless in my lap. The silence in the room was heavy, each tick of the clock reverberating through the stillness. The lingering scent of lavender from the night before mixed with the faint traces of wood from the old furniture, a comforting yet bitter reminder of the space I now occupied without Lilly.

It's been days since she'd left, and with every passing moment, the tumult of emotions crashed against me like waves against a rocky outcrop. Kael, seated nearby, shifted closer. His warmth brushed against my side as if a gentle reminder that I wasn't alone. He glanced at me, his eyes keen and understanding.

"You're lost in thought again," he remarked. "Yeah, just a bit," I murmured, pulling my knees up and wrapping my arms around them. The cozy black knit of my sweater warmed me against the chill in the air, but nothing could thaw the growing sense of dread in the pit of my stomach.

Today, we were meeting with River, Karrie, and Alistair. The Priestess, the Empress, and the Emperor. Each title held meanings I scarcely understood.

I peeked at Kael, his expression a mixture of support and silent strength, but I still couldn't shake the sense of being lost.. Lilly had spoken of the coven's roles as if they were vital strands weaving the fabric of our community, their purpose lending stability to the chaos that swirled around us. But right now, I'm untethered.

"I just... I don't know anything about any of this," I finally admitted, my voice barely above a whisper. Nervous energy coursed through me as I bit my lip. "What if I don't fit in? I never expected to be here, and I certainly didn't think I'd be joining a coven."

His smile widened, and he shifted again, his shoulder nudging mine. "You're not alone in that," he said. "We're all learning here. River and the others know a lot more about what it means to be a part of this coven, and they want to help you."

I leaned back slightly against him, appreciating the quiet strength he offered. "But what if I'm just...not good enough?" I added, my voice cracking just a bit. "What if, now that I have my body back, they decide I don't belong? I know nothing."

"That's why we're here. To help you understand and grow into your new life," He assured me. I leaned back, the edge of the bed digging into my thighs as I took in his words. "I want to," I replied, glancing down at the floor.

"It's just a lot to process. I guess I'll never get to go back to my old life, huh?" My voice cracked slightly at the end, an echo of the past I wasn't ready to relinquish. He shook his head, the gentle movement causing a strand of his golden hair to fall over his brow. "Not unless you can turn back time and stop everything from happening. But that's not how fate works."

I let out a heavy sigh, each breath doused with resignation. Deep down, I knew I couldn't go back to the way things were. Lilly's sacrifice had forever altered my life. I nodded slowly.

"For now, let's head to the meeting hall. They're probably waiting on us," Kael said, rising to his feet. I followed suit, pushing myself off the bed, the cool air brushing against my skin.

As I straightened, the heaviness of the situation settled in. Each step toward the meeting room bore down on me as if I were marching to an interrogation. The hallway stretched before us, the pictures of past heroes and echoes of laughter that felt distant yet close, like a dream fading with the dawn.

The walls closed in around me, and I sensed that strange, vibrating sensation in the pit of my stomach. Apprehension, perhaps? I shoved it aside, dismissing it as I tried to focus on the task ahead. "It's just a meeting," I murmured under my breath, but it sounded more like a mask to convince myself than a statement of fact.

As we approached the massive wooden doors of the meeting hall, the aged oak grain was rough under my fingertips as I brushed against it. Kael paused, casting me a sidelong glance. "Breathe, Em. Everything's going to be okay."

I inhaled deeply, the air tinged with the scent of incense. A heady concoction of sandalwood and something floral that swirled through the air clung to my senses. The sound of muffled voices drifted through the door. As we stepped into the meeting hall, the atmosphere shifted instantly. The space was alive, charged with an ongoing energy.

River, Karrie, and Alistair were already gathered around a large oval table, its surface polished to a warm sheen that reflected the flickering candlelight from ornate sconces lining the walls. They looked up as we entered, expressions mingling with concern and curiosity. "Emma, it's good to see you back to yourself. Although, I wish it were under better circumstances," River said, her voice smooth but heavy with meaning. She leaned forward slightly, her auburn hair catching the light.

"Thank you," I replied, my voice small against the vastness of the room. "Yes, we're truly sorry about everything that's happened," Karrie added, her tone softening as she reached out, brushing her fingers along a small crystal vial on the table.

"But it seems you've become a permanent fixture in our lives." I offered a timid smile. "It appears so. Thanks to Lilly." River nodded, her eyes filled with a depth of understanding.

"Lilly may have been a mess, but she made a huge sacrifice. And I believe she would be proud of you." The sincerity in her words washed over me. "Thank you," I finally managed.

"Now, I think we should begin with your training," River continued, her voice shifting to one of purpose. "You have a unique situation. Kael told us about your ability to use magic even when you weren't in your body, and now..." She paused, glancing at the others.

"You have a combined power of Lilly's magic and your own. We're not sure how this will turn out, if I may be so bold to say."

"We need to teach you how to wield this power," Alistair interjected, as he leaned back, running a hand through his messy, dark hair. "Lilly has already taught you the basics, but with your newfound strength, we'll have to start from scratch." I nodded, feeling the gravity of their intentions sink in.

"That makes sense," I said, trying to keep my voice steady. "I want to be able to honor her memory. I owe it to her, to all of you." Karrie smiled, the amber light catching in her fiery red hair like a halo. "We'll be right beside you through it all, Em. Together, we'll handle whatever comes next." As they began discussing the details of my training, I took in the meeting room. A picture on the wall caught my eye. It was an intricate illustration of the elements intertwined. Fire, water, earth, and air.

A reminder of the balance I would need to maintain. "We want to initiate you into the coven and celebrate your induction as the new 'Star,'" Karrie said, her warm smile lighting up the room. I took a deep breath, my mind turning over her statement.

This was a big step, and without Lilly here, it was as if I were stepping onto a tightrope without a safety net. "I would love to be a part of the coven," I said slowly, "but I think it's too soon to celebrate. Without Lilly, it feels wrong. Like I'm just taking her place, and I don't deserve that." Karrie sighed, nodding in understanding.

"You're not taking Lilly's place. You're your own person, and she would want you to continue living your life. To learn and grow as a witch and as a person. You're special, and you have a gift. That gift came from Lilly. And It would be an honor to have you as part of our coven. As for the celebration, it's not really a party. It's more of a ritual to bring you into the fold."

Hesitance tormented me like a persistent little creature. In the back of my mind, I could almost hear Lilly's voice encouraging me.

As if she were saying, "Go for it, Em." With a reluctant sigh, I agreed. "Okay, let's do it." Karrie beamed. "Wonderful. It'll be tonight as the moon will be full." I nodded, a smile creeping onto my face.

"Thank you. I really appreciate it." She nodded and stood up, brushing off her jeans with a smirk. "I think we're done here."

"If you'd like, Alistair is heading to the training rooms, or you could join me for lunch instead?" I hesitated. The offer was tempting. And I had always gotten along well with Karrie, but the thought of practicing magic with Alistair had my heart racing with excitement. "If it's okay with you, I'd like to start working with Alistair," I replied, carefully weighing my words.

Her smile widened, a hint of understanding in her eyes. "Of course." We made our way to the hallway, the polished stone floors reflecting the light filtering through the tall, arched windows adorned with intricate stained glass. I turned toward Alistair, who leaned casually against the wooden doorframe, looking every bit the part of the Emperor card.

"Lead the way." With a smirk, he turned and strode down the hallway, his footsteps echoing off the high ceilings, which were carved with delicate patterns resembling swirling vines and stars. The grand architecture of the coven was an enchanting mix of medieval charm and modern flair, with exposed beams, stone accents, and an atmosphere that was alive with magic.

We approached the spiral staircase, its dark wood and iron railings spiraled up like a swirling viper. I followed closely behind. At the top of the stairs, Alistair walked to the end of the hall, then turned right, opening a heavy oak door. I stepped in behind him and stumbled a bit, taken aback. The entire training room had completely transformed. Gone were the plush carpet and mismatched chairs. The room now had stark white walls that appeared to pulse with energy.

The space resembled a large gym filled with training equipment—a balance beam, a high bar, and a series of mats laid out in the center. Sunlight streamed in through the frosted glass windows, making the room feel bright and invigorating.

"What happened?" I asked, wide-eyed. Alistair turned to me, a playful grin on his face. "It changes depending on what we need."

"Wow." I was at a loss for words. I had no idea magic could completely change an entire room.

"I know, it's a lot to take in, but you'll get used to it," he said, his tone casual as he walked to the center of the room. "So, what do I do?"

I glanced around, still soaking up the modifications. "Let's start with some warm-ups, then I want to see what you can do so I know where to begin," he said, motioning for me to follow him to the mats. "Alright, I'm ready," I replied, an eager grin spreading across my face.

After several hours of training, I pushed my limits as we dived deeper into the elemental exercises. He guided me through agility drills, weaving between cones that he conjured as we went. Each sprint and maneuver lingered, as if another weight had been added to my shoulders, making my body burn and adrenaline spike.

"Alright, let's try summoning some water," he said, a playful grin on his face as he pointed to a small fountain that shimmered in the corner of the training room. "To connect with it, you'll need to chant the words." I took a deep breath. "What are the words?"

"Just remember, the incantation is only part of it. You need to carry the intention in your heart," he explained. "Say, 'Aqua fluit ad me.' It means 'water flows to me.'" Standing a few feet away from the fountain, I closed my eyes, imagining the water rising to me, flowing like a gentle stream.

"Aqua fluit ad me." A small ripple stirred on the surface of the water, and I noticed a brief connection. A flicker of energy that surged through me. But then it sputtered out. No stream materialized. "Close. You sensed it, right?" Alistair leaned forward slightly.

"Yeah, but I didn't get it to work," I admitted. "Let me try again." This time, I focused harder. "Aqua fluit ad me!" Again, nothing happened. The fountain remained still, the water unyielding.

I couldn't help the groan escaping my lips as I raked a hand through my hair. "Why isn't this working?"

"It takes time, Em. You haven't built your bond yet. Let's try setting an intention. Visualize yourself standing in a flowing river, feeling the water all around you."

"Let that image guide your chant." I took a deep breath, picturing myself standing in a cool, shallow river. I repeated the incantation, pouring my feelings of peace, confidence, and flow into the words. "Aqua fluit ad me." This time, the fountain pulsed, the water rising up a few inches. Alistair stepped closer, his expression serious.

"Remember, control is key to creating magic. Just like in life, balance is everything. If you focus on failure, you'll lose sight of your potential." I sighed. I was expecting something more dramatic. "It feels like I'm stuck."

"Every challenge is a stepping stone. You did well for your experience. Let's move on." Alistair shifted from foot to foot, his voice softening. "Let's focus on fire. It's a different kind of magic, built on passion and heat."

With each attempt, it was as if I were climbing mountains. Yet through it all, Alistair stood patiently guiding me. As the sun dipped lower outside, the shadows of the training room grew longer. "Let's call it a day," He finally said.

"You've done remarkably well, despite the hiccups." I smiled, panting but more optimistic, "Thanks. I appreciate it. I guess I am making some progress." He nodded. "Trust me, every storm has its silver lining. You're on the path to discovering the depths of your strength."

However, as we gathered our things, worry took hold. "What if Xander finds a way to breach our defenses?"

"I don't think he has. And honestly, I doubt he could figure it out," he reassured me. I sighed, pinching the bridge of my nose. "I hope you're right."

Alistair paused thoughtfully as he was gathering supplies. "You know, it's strange without Lilly here. You both were opposites, yet perfectly balanced. It's a shift seeing you, but not having that dynamic."

"Yeah, it's as if I'm living a double life. One where I'm me, and the other is her," I sighed, letting the weight of that thought settle in my chest. "She was always the happy, snarky one. Fearless, bold, and vibrant. And I'm the quiet, shy introvert who never leaves my home." He glanced at me, expression softening.

"You've been changing, though. You're still shy and quiet, but you're not as afraid anymore. You stand up for yourself, and you're becoming more confident."

"I guess," I said, shoving my hands into my pockets. "I just wish it didn't have to be this way. That she didn't have to sacrifice herself. I'm sure there were other options... right?"

He frowned, his brow knitting together in thought. "I'm not sure. She never gave us enough time to figure it out. But fate has a funny way of pushing people toward their paths. Maybe it was just her way of setting things right."

"Yeah, maybe..." I murmured. We left the training hall, our footsteps echoing softly on the floor as we made our way back toward the common room. "Are you hungry? Because I could use a bite to eat," Alistair suggested, glancing sideways at me with a playful glint in his eyes. "And we could go to the market instead of the dining hall."

"Sure, that sounds nice. I'd like to see more of the Mystic Hollows. I didn't see much of it in my own head." He smirked. "I'm sure there's plenty to show you." As we stepped out into the chilly night air, the stars twinkled above. Casting a gentle glow on the cobblestone streets that wound their way through the heart of Mystic Hollows.

"Wow, it's beautiful out here," I marveled. The air was fresh, mingled with scents of blooming jasmine and the crispness of impending autumn. It's weird knowing I was still in Weathersfield, yet existing in a haven hidden within magic.

We walked down the path, passing colorful shops and enchanting buildings. Each had a distinct character. One glowed softly from within, while another had walls adorned with shimmering crystals that sparkled like stars.

A nearby vendor caught my eye. A woman with silver hair. She was selling charms that floated in midair, their glow illuminating her face. I stopped, enchanted. "What are those?"

"Those are luck charms," He explained casually. "They say they can bring good fortune when worn, or even just kept nearby. And in a way, they do work." I watched as she twirled her fingers, and the charms danced in the air, creating a melodic chime.

"That's incredible." We continued, passing a shop where a young man was selling hand-painted potions, the colors shifting beautifully under the starlight. "Look," Alistair said, pointing. "Those are mood potions. Each color corresponds to a different emotion—happy, calm, energized—you name it."

I raised my eyebrows in surprise. "So you could drink a potion if you were down and suddenly be cheerful?"

"Exactly," he replied with a grin. "Though I wouldn't recommend chugging them, or you might be bouncing off walls. Think of it as an energy drink with added mood effects."

"This place is amazing. I can't believe I lived here for months and didn't know it existed." Alistair nodded. "There are many secrets we keep to ourselves. If we share them with outsiders, it could cause... problems."

"I guess I could see that," I said, shaking my head slightly. "I can only imagine the trouble Xander would stir up if he got in."

"Exactly," Alistair nodded. "That's why most coven members live here. We have rules and guidelines to keep everyone safe and sound."

"And the punishments are pretty harsh, right?" I asked, raising an eyebrow. "They are," he replied, his voice serious. "The safety of the coven and the town are the top priority."

"That's good to know," I said, feeling a sense of reassurance as we continued along the winding path. As I looked around, people were walking about, chatting and laughing easily. It was like a normal day in a small town. If you ignore the magical elements.

After a brief stroll, we stopped in front of a charming restaurant. The dimly lit sign above the door read.

"The Crescent Moon Cafe." Its lettering curved like the moon itself. "Is this it?" I asked, peering at the soft, welcoming glow spilling out into the evening air. "Yep! It's one of my favorite places," Alistair said. "The food is amazing." He opened the door, ushering me inside.

"Ladies first." I smiled, stepping into the warmly lit space. The decor was charmingly rustic, with brick walls and local paintings. A few other patrons were scattered around, engaged in hushed conversations, their laughter mingling with the gentle clinking of silverware on plates.

A waitress approached us. On her left wrist was a tattoo of a flourishing tree filled with disks and fruit, along with the number 'X' above it.

"Good evening. I'm Valarie, or Val for short. I'll be your server today. Can I start you off with something to drink?"

"I'll just have water with lemon, please," I replied, glancing at the menu. "Alright, and how about you?" She turned to Alistair, her notepad at the ready. "I'll take a coffee, black with sugar," he said, his eyes still scanning the menu. "Sure thing. I'll be right back with those," Val said with a warm smile before gliding away effortlessly.

"What do you recommend?" I asked, glancing over at Alistair. "Everything here is good, but I really love their pot pie."

"That sounds delicious," I said, feeling my mouth water a little just at the thought. "It is. Definitely one of their best sellers," he added, leaning in slightly. As I took in my surroundings, the atmosphere enveloped me. The soft lighting highlighted the wooden beams across the ceiling, creating an intimate space.

Just then, Val returned, placing our drinks on the table. The fresh scent of lemon mingled with the robust aroma of the coffee. "Here you go. Water with lemon for you, and black coffee with sugar for you."

"Thanks," I said, taking a sip of the chilled water, the citrusy zing refreshing against my palate. "Now, have you decided what you want to eat?" Val asked cheerfully, her pen poised over her notepad. "Yeah, I'll take the cheeseburger with fries. And a side of ranch, please," I said, my mouth watering at the thought of greasy, melty goodness.

"No problem. And you, sir?" she turned toward Alistair. "I'll have the Reuben, with a side of fries as well," he said, giving her a confident nod. "Perfect. I'll have that right out for you guys," she replied, flashing a bright smile before making her way back to the kitchen. Once she left, we settled into a comfortable silence for a moment.

I all but melted into the cozy booth, a feeling of contentment washing over me. "So, what are your plans for tomorrow?" Alistair asked, clearing his throat. I shrugged. "I'm not really sure.

I was hoping to get some more training in, maybe swing by the healer's office and observe for a while. Everything was still so new, and I needed to figure out how to manage it all." He nodded in understanding. "I get that. It's a lot to take in. But I know you'll do great. You're a natural. You've got a big heart and the ability to see the good in people. No doubt you'll make a fine leader one day."

My cheeks flushed as I glanced down at my hands. "Thanks. That really means a lot coming from you. I just hope I can live up to everyone's expectations."

Val returned, placing our steaming plates down in front of us. "Here you go. Enjoy. Let me know if you need anything," she chirped before disappearing. We dug into our meals, savoring the delicious food. Each bite of the cheeseburger was an explosion of flavors—juicy beef, melted cheese, crisp lettuce, and tangy pickles. The fries were golden and perfectly crispy, especially with the ranch. It was a nice shift from the tension and uncertainty I'd felt in the last few days.

After we finished eating, we made our way back to the coven's main house. The energy there was intense as everyone pitched in, scurrying about. I jumped in to help where I could, tidying up the common room. It felt good to be part of the hustle, contributing to something larger than myself.

When all the preparations were complete, we gathered in a circle of stones outside the garden. A gentle breeze rustled the leaves overhead. I stood in the center, feeling every pair of eyes on me, a familiar weight pressing against my chest.

It reminded me of when I first returned to my body. Only this time, it was lighter, almost buoyant. Across the circle, I caught Kael's encouraging smile, which gave me a boost of confidence. The members of the coven held hands, forming a ring around me.

The warmth of their magic enveloped me, reinforcing my energy. Then Kadence began the chant. "In the darkness, there is light. In the void, there is love. We call upon the stars to guide us through this night. To bring forth the blessings of the moon, the sun, and the star."

As the others joined in, repeating the words, their voices rose and fell, intertwining into a hauntingly beautiful melody. I closed my eyes, letting the rhythm wash over me. The chanting resonated deep within me, filling me with a sense of calm and connection.

I could feel something akin to electricity tingling across my skin, like a gentle caress of magic. As the chant grew louder, the energy seemed to shimmer, swirling in a mist of colors both vibrant and soft. I felt intertwined with each person in the circle, sharing their hopes and fears. But then, slowly, an odd feeling crept in.

I sensed an underlying tension emanating from some members of the coven, a mixture of anger and bitterness that curled around us like a dark cloud. I tried to shake it off, but it only grew stronger. Looking around, I searched for the source.

My gaze caught several members glancing at me with suspicion, their expressions clouded with disdain. What is going on? Why are they looking at me like that?

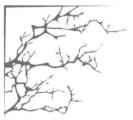

The Last Stand

Xander

A veil of fog rolled through the streets, wrapping the town in shadows as I stalked through the darkness. I paused beneath the skeletal branches of an ancient oak—our spot. Its roots coiled through the earth like a serpent buried deep in its soil.

The moon hung high above, observing silently as I clenched my fists, breathing in the broken promises and memories that swirled around me. For too long, I had remained in the shadows, watching as the humans lived their mundane lives, blissfully ignorant of the magic lurking beyond their world.

Tonight, I would shatter that illusion. Tonight, they would learn that they lived in a fragile bubble—one that I had the power to burst. With a flick of my wrist, I summoned my magic, channeling it into the ground beneath my feet.

The earth trembled, and flames ignited at my command, roaring to life like a beast released against the backdrop of the night.

The first fire crackled hungrily, consuming the old barn, its flames reaching for the sky with a chaotic hunger "Let chaos reign," I murmured, losing myself in the dance of the flames that illuminated the woods. The heat washed over me, a wicked thrill surging through my veins. This was just the beginning. This town would burn—just as she would have wanted it.

A stark reminder of betrayal, that's all. As the flames raged, I slipped through the shadows, pressing deeper into the town and feeding the fire with tendrils of magic.

Shouts erupted from nearby homes, the commotion rising as people stumbled into the streets, wide-eyed and panicked. The confusion and fear felt like sweet music to my ears, an uplifting crescendo pushing me forward.

Power pulsed through me as I pushed my energy into the foundation of Weathersfield, sending people running in every direction. From the barn, I leaped toward the bustling market, igniting stalls with ease, reveling in the flames that surged to engulf everything in sight.

A part of me thrived on their terror, feeding off it like a drug. It tinged the air with excitement, intoxicated by the dark tendrils of destruction unfurling toward the horizon.

Homes crackled and crumbled, roofs sagging under the weight of the flames. The scent of burning wood hung thick and sweet, a heady perfume of loss and revenge. Nothing could stop me—not now. Lillith might have thought she had the upper hand, but this was my moment to remind her just how wrong she was.

If a little chaos and fear were what it took, then so be it. She'd see it soon enough. If I happened to take out the coven in the process, all the better. Suddenly, voices beckoned from beyond the flames, and I turned to find a trio approaching through the haze.

A woman with long brunette hair walked with purpose, sporting the number X above a tattoo of a tree adorned with discs and fruits. The guy beside her, with raven-black hair, moved confidently, his own tattoo depicting a single disc perched on a pedestal—the number I clearly visible.

And then there was the imposing figure in the middle, radiating power with a crumbling tower tattoo, the number XVI looming over it. "Come to crash my party?" A half-smirk played on my lips as I surveyed them, the flames casting flickering shadows that danced like whispers in the dark. The brunette squared her shoulders, her voice steady despite the chaos. "We sensed a disturbance, and we were concerned."

"Looks like you've been busy," the dark-haired guy chimed in, a grin creeping onto his face as he surveyed my handiwork, eyes glimmering with excitement.

"Have you come to stop me?" I asked, curiosity dripping from my words, raising an eyebrow in challenge. "Not at all. We're here to help." The second guy shrugged, his confidence stark against the tension in the air.

Skepticism whispered at the back of my mind, and I narrowed my eyes, sizing them up. "Why should I trust you?" The third one stepped forward, his aura encroaching on the heat, radiating from my flames like a cool breeze. It sent shivers down my spine, raising the hairs on my neck with immediate wariness.

"Because the minor arcana are sick of the coven looking down on them. And personally? I want Lilly gone. This whole charade of her playing as Emma is bullshit, and everyone in the coven is buying it." He extended his hand confidently, a mix of challenge and invitation hanging in the air

"I'm Dom. This is Valarie and Felix. We want to join you. What do you say?" I studied the trio closely, gauging their intentions. In a flash, I stepped forward, seizing Dom by the throat, the flames momentarily casting his face in harsh light.

"You ever call her a bitch again, and I'll snap your neck. Clear?" His eyes widened, a flash of acknowledgment crossing his features as the sharp smell of sulfur mingled with the smoke.

The air crackled with an undercurrent of tension, a power struggle ending with his reluctant nod. "Understood," he ground out, a mix of defiance and respect flickering in his gaze. "Good." I released him, smirking as he stumbled back, a newfound wariness overtaking him.

As they prepared to disappear into the night, shadows blending with the dark, a grin tugged at my lips. Soon, Lilly. I'm coming for you.

Emma

Training sessions blurred together—a whirlwind of meetings with the Major Arcana and the minor arcanum, vibrant yet tangled in an awkwardness that was way too familiar. It was like being the new kid at school where no one wanted to talk to you.

My gaze slipped over to Cassie, sprawled back in her chair with a relaxed confidence. Arms crossed, a quirky smirk plastered on her face, she was practically oozing chill vibes. "Are you ready, or do I need to perform a dramatic spell to motivate you?" She winked, the lightness in her tone a hopeful counterbalance to my rising tension.

"Very funny," I shot back, rolling my eyes, but a smile tugged at my lips despite myself. Her humor was a welcome distraction—a little spark of light amid the storm churning inside me—like the Death card, bringing transformation and change with a side of flair.

But that spark dimmed as she locked her gaze on mine, concern darkening her playful demeanor. "Seriously, though."

She leaned in, voice dropping to a hushed intensity. "Find your center. Okay? Hold the rune stone tight and draw on your power. Have it flow through you like a wave. Nodding, I pressed the rune stone against my palm, its cool, smooth surface grounding me. "What now?"

"Now, close those lovely eyes of yours," she instructed, nudging me gently. "Concentrate. Channel all your magic and let it mingle with the stone." Shutting my eyes, I sank into the depths of my own mind, focusing on the stone. It began to pulse in my hand, a warm, gentle rhythm that synced with the beat of my heart.

"Good, keep going," she urged, her enthusiasm sparking energy in the air. "Think about her. Dig deep into those mushy memories. What did she teach you? How did she make you feel?"

I let out a deep breath, the chaotic memories of the day Lilly entered my life—the frantic moments in the ER, panic gripping me like a vice. But Lilly hadn't been frightening. No, she was a mischievous whirlwind, turning my fears to ashes with her unstoppable spirit.

She kept nudging me—pushing me to get up, to live, even while I was drowning in grief. A chuckle bubbled up within me at Cassie's unique way of motivating me. "Alright, I remember those nights she'd distract me while I was grieving over my parents. She was relentless but so present, teasing but always pushing me to keep moving again."

"Good, keep digging," Cassie urged, eyes alight with encouragement. The stone glowed brighter with each revelation, a vibrant pulse building around me like a vortex, drawing me further into those feelings. "Lilly, I forgive you. I don't blame you," I whispered, the weight of those words heavy with the shared experiences we'd endured together.

Memories flooded my mind, and I knew it was finally time to say goodbye. The final goodbye. With a tremor in my voice, I murmured, "You were there for me when no one else was, thank you."

And then, without warning, light exploded around me, engulfing me in a blinding blaze. I felt myself being lifted, suspended in some luminous void, when I heard it—a soft echo of a voice that sent my heart racing. "Thank you, Em. I'm sorry, and I love you.

I'll be seeing you again soon." A bittersweet smile formed on my lips. It was Lilly. But what did she mean by "I'll be seeing you again soon"? Just as the weight of her words settled in, a loud crash jolted me back to reality. Muffled screams echoed through the air.

"What the hell?" I murmured, heart pounding as I rushed to the window. I pressed my forehead against the cold glass, panic surging through me like a live wire.

The garden below was a nightmare, alive with chaos, flames reaching hungrily for the night sky as smoke spiraled upward, twisting like dark spirits desperate for escape.

"Cassie!" I screamed, catching sight of her wide-eyed silhouette, horror etched across her face. With a burst of adrenaline, she dashed out of the room. Stunned for a heartbeat, confusion roiling in my chest, instinct kicked in. I sprinted after her, heart pounding wildly as I reached the top of the stairs. My stomach dropped.

A masked figure lunged toward her, shadows flickering like ominous wings around it. "Cassie, look out!" I shouted, my voice slicing through the chaos. She spun on her heels and shoved the figure back. But she staggered onto the landing, out of sight. Fear twisted my gut. As I scanned the foyer below, dread washed over me again—another figure loomed like a dark cloud.

"Dom?" I stuttered, the name tasting bitter on my tongue. His grin was sadistic, a predator in the frenzy of the hunt. "Shame you had to pretend to be Emma, but I know your secret, Lillith," he sneered, his words cutting through the fog in my mind. "Justice and chaos will be served today."

Lillith? My brain spun, struggling to understand. Did this guy really think she was still here? It was as if the ground rolled beneath me, shadows choking out hope. "You're delusional!" I shouted, rejection swelling in me. "I have no idea what you're talking about!"

"Stop. It's insulting to play dumb," he spat, laughter dripping with malice. "I've known since the beginning." A wave of dread settled like a stone in my stomach. I opened my mouth to defend myself, but the words tangled in confusion, leaving me adrift in a storm of thoughts.

His taunts stabbed at me, slicing through the overwhelming noise around us. "I hope Xander locks you away where you never see the light of day again," he cackled, each word robbing me of whatever courage I had left.

Then, like a shadow slipping into darkness, he vanished, and my instincts screamed to follow him, to confront him. But I hesitated, fear rooting me in place. Thunder echoed overhead, rumbling like a warning. I tilted my head back, wide-eyed, as a jagged bolt of lightning tore through the roiling black clouds above, illuminating the chaos.

The acrid smoke thickened the air, curling into my chest and forcing a sputter from my lungs. "Help!" The word rang out, frantic and raw, cutting through the suffocating haze. I desperately scanned the area for a glimpse of Cassie. "Someone help me!"

Her voice rang out again, and before logic could catch up, my body reacted, sprinting down the steps. The flames crackled nearby, a scorching rhythm pulsing through the air like a malevolent heartbeat. "Please!"

I closed my eyes for a heartbeat, straining to listen. "Cassie!" I shouted, adrenaline roaring in my ears as the sound of structures breaking sent panic through my veins.

"Over here!" Her voice was strained, laced with a fear that twisted my gut. "Where are you?" I called out, the smoke too thick to cut through. "I'm here!" Each cough was like knives stabbing into my lungs, but I followed her voice, my instincts guiding me.

"Keep talking!" I urged, needing her to guide me. "I'm here!" Holding my breath, I reached out, fingers trembling as I searched for her hand. "Where are you?" I rasped, desperation clawing at me. "I'm here." Finally, her fingers brushed against mine, relief flooding my senses, and I clasped her hand tightly.

"We have to get out of here," Cassie insisted. I nodded, even though she couldn't see it. "Follow me." I tugged her along through the blazing garden, but then she paused, her grip tightening. "Hold on, Em." Her gaze shifted, a spark of intensity igniting through the chaos. "Guardian of the grove, hear my plea.

Set your sacred water free. From evil-doers' hands, be washed free." The air shimmered, electrified with energy, and suddenly, the fountain roared to life. The statue atop it had awakened, wand raised to the heavens.

A torrent of water surged forth, cascading down in a dazzling wave of gold and silver. I stood there, stunned, as the magical deluge enveloped the flames, snuffing them out with fierce intensity. "What. Was. That?" I whispered. "That was amazing! How did you know to do that?"

"The statue was enchanted, just in case," Cassie said. "Now he'll protect the garden. Come on! We've got to get inside and activate the other protections." I led the way, the others trailing behind us, their footsteps echoing in the charged atmosphere.

Bursting into the meeting hall of the coven, the sight that met us sent a chill racing down my spine. Four figures loomed, backlit by swirling flames. Xander leaned against the far wall, arms crossed, resolve hardening his features.

Dom stood next to him, eyes narrowed, while Valarie stepped forward, radiating fury. Felix hung back, caught in a web of tension. "How could you?" I breathed, disbelief flooding my voice as I stepped closer. Valarie lunged forward, tension crackling off her like a live wire. "We want the injustice to stop.

We want you to leave, Lillith!" She spat the last word, each syllable overflowing with contempt. "Wait, what? She's dead, gone!" I stammered, trying to make sense of the chaos. "You're all delusional."

"No," Valarie shot back, her voice knife-like. "You're just conning the major arcane members into turning against us." My throat tightened, a tempest of confusion and indignation boiling inside me.

"Because you're not from here!" she shouted, gesturing as if trying to shatter a glass pane. "You brought in darkness, and now suddenly you're the star card? It's bullshit." Shocked, I struggled to respond, but words eluded me. "Em!" Lillith's voice rang in my mind like a bell. "You need to cast a protection circle now!"

"Lillith?" I called, but she didn't respond, her magic mingling with mine, intoxicating and powerful. "Now, Em!" I jumped back, hands moving instinctively, magic surging within me.

167

"In the name of the goddess, I call upon the guardians of the watchtower of the north. I call upon the guardians of the watchtower of the south. I call upon the guardians of the watchtower of the east. I call upon the guardians of the watchtower of the west. Four corners of our sanctuary, four winds that blow, four seasons of the year, I conjure thee. I command the elements to bind us, to protect us, to keep us safe. Let no evil come within our circle. This space is consecrated and protected. So mote it be!"

Energy surged forward, the air pulsating around me, the earth beneath my feet vibrating.

Water surged with a gentle pulse, and flames danced at my fingertips. The guardians arose, pulsing through the very essence of the elements. "You're not welcome here," I declared, fury igniting within me as I aimed my magic at them. "Get out!" I shouted, and Xander was thrown back, crashing against the wall.

He climbed to his feet, wiping the blood from his lip, laughter echoing like the tolling of a cruel bell. "Lillith left you because she wants to be with me again! I will do her justice. I will give her it all!" His voice crescendoed into a frenzied scream as he unleashed a scorching stream of magic aimed straight at my circle.

Heat enveloped me, an intense wave searing my skin, squeezing the breath from my lungs. I collapsed to my knees, the ground cool against my shaky body. The world tilted dangerously, but I couldn't let go—every life here was intertwined with my own. If I faltered, we would all fall.

"Em! Chant with me!" Cassie's voice cut through the haze of pain, grounding me. I felt Kael, Orion, and River surrounding me, their energy steadying my racing heart. "What the hell are you doing?" Xander yelled, disbelief flooding his tone. "She doesn't know magic! She's useless!"

"That's where you're wrong, Xander," I shot back, grit filling my voice as I stood tall again.

"We are a coven. We work together. Each of us brings something special to the table. It's our combined magic, our shared knowledge—this is why we've survived everything. Lillith thought you were a lost cause. She sacrificed herself for me. She gave me her strength, her love, her magic. Do you honestly think that wielding power makes you important? That your brute force makes you superior? You're dead wrong! Because without the rest of us, you would be nothing!"

I drew from the essence of the four elements—fire, earth, water, and air. Instantly, the heat washed over me, merging with an electric crackle in the air. The coolness of the wind swirled around my body, and the earth beneath my feet churned like a restless beast.

"Emma! Banish him now!" Lillith's voice roared to life, a lifeline slicing through the chaos. She had been with me this whole time, guiding me, lending her strength even from the shadows.

I dropped my protective circle and leaped forward, harnessing every ounce of might I had. A loud, heart-wrenching crack split the air as I pushed against Xander, the force rippling outward, slamming into him like a cannonball. He staggered back, but I fought with everything I had.

And then—boom—a dazzling flash of white light erupted between us, blinding and searing, and in an instant, he was gone, a dark presence banished at last. Panting, I stood there, disbelief washing over me as I gazed at the empty space where he had just been. The eyes of the coven were locked on me.

Some filled with admiration, others with confusion. Those who had followed Xander were on their knees, heads bowed in shame, remnants of their power echoing their weakened choices. Kael stepped closer, gaze intense as he locked eyes with me. "What do we do with them?" I asked cautiously.

"We need to bind their magic and banish them. It's the only way," he said, voice grim, old scars of loyalty and betrayal glimmering in his eyes. A few of the former members flinched at his words.

Dom's eyes flashed with defiance, inner turmoil raging. "No! That's not right." I shot back, voice fierce. "They were misguided, but they should get a chance. If we cast them out, we're no better than Xander."

"What other choice do we have?" River pressed, stepping forward. "What if they decide to cause even more harm?"

"We won't, if you hear us out." Valarie's voice was steady amidst the rising tension. "Emma." Dom called out, earnestness gleaming in his eyes

"I'm sorry. I wasn't thinking straight. I promise I'll make it up to you. I give up my birthright, my card, and my magic. I just... want to live a normal life. I studied him, the weight of his words palpable. In an instant, his hand hovered over his tattoo, whispering an incantation that sent shivers down my spine.

A moment later, the tattoo vanished, leaving bare skin beneath the silvery moonlight. My heart sank at the sight. "Dom, no. I don't want you to give up your magic," I said, my voice trembling as the thought of him walking away from such an essential part of himself constricted my chest. He held my gaze, his expression unwavering, and replied, "I don't deserve it."

I took a step back, feeling a mix of disbelief and desperation. "Honestly, it doesn't bring me joy anymore. I'm done with it. All this does is make me angry." His brow furrowed, a look of determination replacing the flicker of doubt I had hoped to see.

River stepped closer, her eyes filled with concern, her brows knitted together in worry. "Are you sure?" she asked cautiously, her voice barely above a whisper.

"Yes. I'm positive," he affirmed, his voice steady but his jaw tense, reinforcing his decision. I could see the resolve in his eyes, but it did little to ease the ache in my heart

"Then it's settled." Kael's voice sliced through the tension. "We accept your resignation. But you cannot stay here. You have to go."

"I understand," Dom spoke quietly, voice cracking slightly as if he were already grieving what he was leaving behind. I watched him turn toward the portal, a part of me hoping he'd change his mind, but he kept walking forward, disappearing into the shadows.

The sun had set hours ago, leaving darkness to cloak the remnants of our battleground. We'd been cleaning up after the attack, the air heavy with the scent of burnt magic—a bitter reminder of the chaos we'd faced.

Miraculously, only a few had sustained injuries, thankfully not serious. But an unsettling silence hung in the air as I realized I could no longer sense Lillith's presence. It was as if she had known what was coming—stepping in just long enough to guide me, then fading away.

Yet, something felt missing, something vital that I couldn't quite grasp. Just then, Cassie approached, her expression unreadable. Instead of speaking, she nodded toward the forest beyond the garden, beckoning me to follow. Confusion swirled within me, but curiosity drove me on as I trailed her.

Then, as we rounded a bend, I stopped dead in my tracks. A familiar figure sat in the distance, backlit by the moon.

Long blonde hair framed her face, and sparkling emerald eyes met mine, an ocean of unspoken emotions swirling within them. I didn't speak; disbelief wrapped around me like a cloak as my mind raced to reconcile what lay before me. She was here. Alive and real.

Slowly, hesitantly, she stood, as if unsure I would welcome her. Taking a deep breath, I closed the distance, feet moving forward despite my shock. Lillith.

The name echoed within me as I walked closer, every fiber screaming to hug her, to confirm that this wasn't some cruel trick.

Finally, I stood before her, reaching out to grasp her hand. Her pulse throbbed beneath my fingers. "How? How are you here?" I managed to choke out, tears of joy and confusion blurring my vision. She reached up to wipe them away, her touch cool against my flushed cheeks. "Em, Hecate decided to give me one more chance at life to do the right thing—to fix the wrongs I'd made. But it comes with a price."

She revealed her wrist, where a tattoo of an inverted star with waves above and a flame below had replaced her old one. "I'm sorry for leaving. It was the hardest decision I ever had to make, but it was the only way to fix what I had done to you. I've received the inverted star card mark.

Until I prove myself, I'll remain tethered with this mark, and my magic will be limited." My mind reeled, emotions in turmoil. I knew what she had sacrificed—her birthright, her legacy, everything.

Words escaped me, so I pulled her into a tight embrace. Moments later, Cassie joined us, and we stood wrapped together. "Whatever you have to go through, you won't be doing it alone," I whispered, my throat tight with emotion.

Lilly nodded, gratitude shimmering in her gaze. "Thank you for understanding." She turned serious, her expression shifting. "I need to tell you something, Em. When I gave you my magic, I gave a part of myself. Now, I can feel our connection. We're in for a hell of a journey ahead. But I'll be here for you."

A smile broke across my face, warmth spreading as her words sank in. The weight of what she said filled me with strength. For the first time, I felt ready to take on the world. I wouldn't be doing it alone. I squeezed her hand. "Let's do this, together."

Milton Keynes UK
Ingram Content Group UK Ltd.
UKHW040809051024
449151UK00001B/61